**Praise for the Tj Jens**

"Daley's characters come to life on the page. Her novels are filled with a little mystery and a little romance which makes for a murderous adventure."

– Tonya Kappes,
*USA Today* Bestselling Author of *Fixin' To Die*

"Daley's mysteries offer as much sizzle and pop as fireworks on a hot summer's day."

– Mary Kennedy,
Author of The Dream Club Mysteries

"I'm a huge fan of Kathi's books. I think I've read every one. Without a doubt, she's a gifted cozy mystery author and I eagerly await each new release!"

– Dianne Harman,
Author of the High Desert Cozy Mysteries

"Intriguing, likeable characters, keep-you-guessing mysteries, and settings that literally transport you to Paradise...Daley's stories draw you in and keep you glued until the very last page."

– Tracy Weber,
Agatha-Nominated Author of the Downward Dog Mysteries

"Daley really knows how to write a top-notch cozy."

– *MJB Reviewers*

"Kathi Daley writes a story with a puzzling cold-case mystery while highlighting...the love of home, family, and good friends."

– *Chatting About Cozies*

# Thanksgiving

**A
TJ JENSEN
MYSTERY**

## IN

# PARADISE

**The Tj Jensen Mystery Series**
**by Kathi Daley**

# Thanksgiving IN PARADISE

A
TJ JENSEN
MYSTERY

## KATHI DALEY

HENERY PRESS

Copyright

THANKSGIVING IN PARADISE
A Tj Jensen Mystery
Part of the Henery Press Mystery Collection

First Edition | October 2019

Henery Press, LLC
www.henerypress.com

This is a work of fiction. Any references to historical events, real people, or real locales are used fictitiously. Other names, characters, places, and incidents are the product of the author's imagination, and any resemblance to actual events or locales or persons, living or dead, is entirely coincidental.

Trade Paperback ISBN-13: 978-1-63511-539-0
Digital epub ISBN-13: 978-1-63511-540-6
Kindle ISBN-13: 978-1-63511-541-3
Hardcover ISBN-13: 978-1-63511-542-0

Printed in the United States of America

*This series is about family and I have a large one.*
*I want to dedicate this book to the entire network of people with*
*whom I share a bloodline and a history.*

## ACKNOWLEDGMENTS

They say it takes a village and I have a great one.

I want to thank all my friends who hang out over at my Kathi Daley Books Group page on Facebook. This exceptional group help me not only with promotion but with helpful suggestion and feedback as well.

I want to thank the bloggers and reviewers who have pretty much adopted me and have helped me to build a fantastic social media presence. I want to thank my support staff including my book club moderator Jayme Maness, my tech guy Bruce Curran, my graphic artist Jessica Fisher, and my editors Randy Ladenheim-Gil and Peggy Hyndman.

I want to thank the entire Henery Press family who have been so incredibly awesome and fun to work with.

And last but certainly not least, I want to thank my super-husband Ken for allowing me time to write by taking care of everything else (and I mean everything).

# CHAPTER 1

Tuesday, October 31

*"You've really improved since we last played, but I can see that you still haven't learned the most effective use your queen."*

*I frowned as I considered the image of the grizzly old man sitting across from me. "My queen is protecting my king."*

*Zachary slid his hand forward, picked up his chess piece, and knocked my queen gently off the board. "Not anymore."*

*I groaned as I realized that he had bested me yet again. "Why are you here?"*

*He chuckled. "Beats me."*

*"You've been dead for four years. You really shouldn't be here. Unless... Am I dead?"*

*"No, you aren't dead."*

*I looked around at the dense fog that surrounded the small table where Zachary and I sat. "Today is Halloween, the anniversary of the day we met. You've been on my mind so I suppose that could explain your presence in my subconscious. I must be sleeping."*

*"Actually, I think you're unconscious."*

*I frowned. "Well, that can't be good."*

*Zachary shrugged and began setting the board up for a new game.*

*I glanced at the gossamer image across from me. "This whole thing is really weird, but I am happy to spend time with you. I've missed our games."*

*"As have I, although we do still have one game left to play."*

"Tj," a voice beckoned. I swatted at the hand on my face as someone outside my dream pulled me out of the fog.

*"Wait,"* I called to Zachary as he began to fade. *"I'm not ready for the dream to end. I didn't have a chance to tell you about Kyle and me."*

"Come on, sweetheart. I need you to wake up."

I fought the voice that pulled me toward it. Not only did I have so many more questions for Zachary, but as my mind cleared, the throbbing in my head and the pain in my leg, became very real. I struggled to stay in the dream, but the voice was too compelling. I silently screamed as I was pulled into a world of hurt, where sirens blared, lights flashed, and the images around me spun like the tilt-a-whirl at the county fair.

"That's it, stay with me," the annoying voice insisted as I struggled against it.

"Kyle?" I croaked.

"No. It's Hunter. Can you tell me where it hurts?"

I opened my eyes just a slit. My face was wet, and there was something heavy on my leg.

"Hunter?" This couldn't be right. Hunter Hanson was one of my very best friends, but he'd been hurt that I'd hooked up with Zachary's grandson, Kyle Donovan, and he hadn't been coming around lately. I supposed I could still be dreaming, although if this was a dream, it was a poor substitute for the calm and peaceful world I'd been forced to leave behind.

"That's right. It's Hunter. I'm going to get you out of here, but I need you to lay perfectly still until I can."

As the last of the fog from the dream faded, I became aware

of the wet ground and the debris around me. It seemed like it must be raining. I could barely make out the images within my line of sight, but I was pretty sure I was inside a building. Or at least I had been inside a building. At this point, all that was left were half collapsed walls. I wanted to ask what in the heck was going on, but I felt my mind drifting back toward the darkness. Maybe I'd just rest for a moment before I tried to figure all of this out.

"Doctor Hanson," a female voice said from somewhere beyond the fog. "The emergency crew are here with a jack. They should have Ms. Jensen free in a matter of minutes."

"That's good news. Do you know what is going on with the other victims?"

"Two are dead, and four are on their way to the hospital."

"Okay. Keep me posted."

Hospital? I played with the concept in my mind. That didn't seem right. I remembered that there was somewhere I needed to be, but I was pretty sure that a hospital had not been involved. Although now that I thought about it, I was beginning to remember the loud noise, bright light, and flash of pain before the world went black.

"Just a few more minutes, sweetheart," Hunter said as he shone a bright light into my eyes.

I tried to speak, but my mouth felt as if it had been stuffed with cotton candy. The fog surrounding me had cleared, and the pain that had been nothing more than an impression was beginning to get very real. "Leg," I groaned.

"Your leg is pinned beneath a beam," Hunter said as he stroked my hair. "The emergency crew will get you free, so just hang in there."

"Beam? Where am I?"

"The town hall. There's been an explosion."

I realized the rain must actually be water from the fire

hoses used to put out the fire. "Kyle?"

"He is being looked after. Now, I need you to try to relax. Just take a deep breath and focus on the sound of my voice."

I felt myself drifting away. Hunter said something I really didn't follow, so I turned my focus toward my dream where visions of Zachary blocked the pain and noise from my mind. I'd first met the elderly Zachary Collins on Halloween night almost eighteen years earlier. My friends had dared me to sneak inside the gated estate where the monster-like recluse lived, knock on the door, and then run away. Never one to turn down a dare, that's what I did. Zachary had caught me, and we'd become close friends. He'd been murdered four years ago, and I'd missed him every day since, so I wasn't at all surprised that it was him I'd hallucinate about if I was, in fact, hallucinating.

*"Zachary, are you still here?" I called into the fog.*

*His image appeared. "You know I am always here, watching out for you, guiding you through life's trials."*

*The fear and pain I'd experienced faded as Zachary held out his hand to me. "Are you sure I'm not dead? Things seem pretty serious back there."*

*"You aren't dead, but death is present. As much as I'd love to keep you here with me, your friends are going to need you. It's time for you to go back and face what you must."*

*"But..."*

"It looks like she is coming to," said a voice somewhere on the other side of the fog. "Her leg is free, and what's left of this building is about to come down. Let's get out of here while we can."

I recoiled in pain as I was lifted onto a backboard. The whirling lights reflecting off the wet surfaces made me woozy, so I closed my eyes. Hunter still clung to my hand, so I squeezed tighter as I rode out the crazy waves of dizziness and nausea.

"She is the last one, so I'll just ride to the hospital with you," I heard Hunter say to someone, I assumed the ambulance driver.

"Sure thing Doctor Hanson. We'll get you there as soon as we're able."

I heard a door slam just seconds before the world around me jerked into motion.

"I think I'm going to be sick," I managed to say as the vehicle transporting me took a sharp corner.

"Take a deep — slow — breath," Hunter said. "We're almost there."

"Almost where?" I struggled to keep my dinner on the inside as the vehicle whipped around yet another corner.

"The hospital," Hunter answered. "Once we arrive, I'm going to need to leave you in order to help the others. How is your leg?"

I moved my leg and wiggled my toes. "Now that the pressure is gone, my leg feels fine." My nausea had passed, so I dared to open my eyes to find Hunter's blue eyes staring into my own.

"I can't know for certain without an x-ray, but it appears as if your leg isn't even broken."

I smiled. "You always did say that I might be small, but I was tough."

"Titanium tough. It isn't everyone who can have a building come down on them and walk away with only a few cuts and bruises."

The remainder of the building coming down made me frown. "Kyle? He was just a few steps in front of me."

Hunter squeezed my hand. "He was taken to the hospital. I don't know his status at this point, but I promise you I'll personally check on him when we get there."

"And the others?"

Hunter shook his head. "I don't know. I stayed behind with

you after the others were transported to the hospital. I'm going to do everything possible to save those I can. The others were closer to the blast, but you don't need to think about that. I want you to try to slow your breathing and calm your mind. Your blood pressure is off the charts. We need to get it down, and for that to happen, you need to relax."

Relax? Was he kidding?

The vehicle stopped, and the back door opened. I watched Hunter as he got up.

"Don't go," I said, suddenly scared of being left alone amongst all the chaos and uncertainty.

"I have to go," he said. "You are going to be fine. I am turning you over to a very capable nurse, and I'll check on you later. I had the hospital call your dad. He's probably already here." Hunter kissed me gently on the lips and then disappeared.

The next few minutes were like a nightmare. Bright lights, people hovering, IV's being inserted even though I was sure that other than having a raging headache, I actually was, as Hunter had promised, just fine. I looked around for my father whose voice I could hear but whose face I couldn't see. I could hear people yelling and running, and smell blood and burnt flesh. It was then that I finally lost the dinner I'd been so valiantly trying to hang onto.

# CHAPTER 2

Thursday, November 2

I clung to my dad's arm as the snow outside a nearby window drifted gently toward the soggy earth. Tears pooled as the funeral director tried to explain the options available to us. I knew there were decisions to be made, but I had to admit I wasn't really listening. I glanced at my best friend, Jenna Elston, who clung to her mother, but they didn't appear to be paying any more attention to the man than I was.

"I think a simple service on Saturday would be best," I heard my dad say. "I spoke to Pastor Dan, and he is available in the afternoon. If you call him, he'll coordinate the specifics with you."

Jenna's mother, Helen Hellerman, had been named as the executor in the last will and testament of her best friend, Harriet Kramer, but given the fact that Helen's new husband was in the hospital clinging to life, she really wasn't in any shape to make decisions. I wanted to do what I could to help, but I wasn't in all that great of shape myself, so I'd enlisted the help of the man who'd always been there for me, my father, Mike Jensen.

"I'll need someone to fill out the paperwork required for the cremation of the remains," the funeral director said.

"Is this something I can do?" Dad asked.

"Yes, that should be fine."

I looked at Jenna. "Why don't you go ahead and take your mom home. The poor thing hasn't slept in days. I'll stay and finish up here, and then I'll call you with the final times and whatnot."

Jenna glanced at Helen. "Okay. Thank you. I think that would be best."

I got up and limped across the room. The leg that had been trapped by a beam from the frame of the building after the explosion that had killed two people and injured four others had left me feeling battered and bruised, but, as Hunter had suspected, I hadn't broken a single bone. The beam had miraculously fallen in such a way that it trapped my leg but did not crush it. I'd been lucky. The other occupants of that room hadn't gotten off so lightly.

My dad seemed to have everything under control with the funeral director, so I decided to walk Jenna and Helen to their car. I said a few words to Jenna, hugged both women, and tucked Helen into her seat before waving them off. I turned to head back into the building when I noticed my grandfather, Ben Jensen, arrive with his best friend, Doc aka Stan Griffin. I paused and waited while they parked.

"You didn't have to come," I said after the men climbed out and headed in my direction. "Dad seems to have everything under control. The funeral will be on Saturday."

Grandpa tightened his lips and furrowed his brow revealing his anger and pain.

"We went by the hospital to check on the others," Doc explained. "Bookman and Hank are still unconscious, but Jeff has been moved out of the ICU and is expected to make a full recovery. The only one we were actually able to speak to was Kyle, who is chomping at the bit to get out of there. From what I understand, he will be released today unless his labs come back less than ideal."

I sighed. "I'd hoped Bookman would be awake by the time I stopped by today. I know the uncertainty is taking its toll on Helen."

"Maybe he will wake up before the end of the day," Grandpa said, taking my hand in his and giving it a squeeze.

"I hope so." I let out a long breath. "I still can't believe that both Lloyd and Harriet are gone. The whole thing seems so pointless."

Grandpa, a tall and sturdy man with white hair and faded blue eyes, walked toward me with outstretched arms. I walked into them, relaxing just a bit as his strong arms tightened around me. I closed my eyes for just a moment as I rested my head on his shoulder. It had been two days since the explosion, but I was still having a hard time coming to grips with the reality of the whole thing. My dad had always told me that when life threw you a curve, the only thing you could do was to deal with each moment as it came. That, I decided, was what I was going to do now.

"Is your dad still inside?" Doc asked.

I nodded and took a step back.

"I guess we'll head in and offer support," Grandpa said.

"Will you let him know that I'm going to head to the hospital? I'm hoping Kyle will be released this afternoon and I want to be there if he is."

"I'll tell him," Grandpa answered in a deep voice that rumbled up from his chest. "Call us when you are able to confirm one way or the other if Kyle will be able to go home today."

I turned my head and kissed Grandpa on his cheek. "I will. Call me if you hear anything. One way or another, we're going to figure out who did this."

I climbed into my car and headed toward the main highway

that ran through town. As I drove to the hospital, I thought about the night of the explosion. It had been Halloween, and Kyle and I had taken my youngest sister, Gracie, and her best friend, Kari, trick or treating. We were halfway across town when Kyle got a text alerting him to an emergency town council meeting. There had been a lot of dishevel in the council ever since Mayor Harper had been killed this past summer, and secret meetings behind closed doors had almost become the norm. Kyle felt that secret meetings violated the implied contract that the council had with the town residents, but there had been a lot of delicate issues that needed to be dealt with since Harper's death, so the secret meetings had continued. By the time we'd handed Gracie and Kari off to Jenna, we'd been late for the meeting, and the other council members had already arrived. Technically, I supposed my presence at the meeting was not allowed since I wasn't a town council member, but Kyle and I had plans that evening, so we figured that if they wanted Kyle's presence, they'd need to deal with my presence, as well. I planned to sit in the back and wait so I hadn't continued on into the room as Kyle headed toward the front of the council chambers. When he was about halfway down the aisle, I heard a loud boom and the next thing I knew, I was playing chess with Zachary.

Harriet, who served as town clerk and the mayor's secretary, sat the closest to the origin of the blast and died immediately as did Lloyd Benson, the council member and developer closest to where she sat. Restaurant owner, Hank Hammond, sat next to Lloyd and was currently clinging to life in the ICU. There was an empty chair next to Hank where Helen's husband, R. L. Hellerman aka Bookman, usually sat, but he was filling in as interim mayor, so he sat in the center of the row which was one seat over from his usual seat. To Bookman's right was the empty seat where Kyle usually sat, and to the right of

Kyle's empty seat sat the newest town council member, Jeff Warren, who took over Doug Conrad's seat when he quit unexpectedly. There was one additional empty seat at the end of the row which was waiting to be filled. The group had decided to wait to fill the seat until a new mayor had been selected.

"Did you take care of everything you needed to?" Kyle asked after I walked into his hospital room with a forced smile on my face.

"We are all set. The funeral for Helen will be on Saturday." I slipped off my shoes, and as carefully as I could so as not to hurt his ribs, two of which had been broken, slipped onto the bed beside him.

"I wish I could have been there to offer support," Kyle said, as I laid my head on his shoulder. I placed a hand on his chest as he carefully wrapped his arms around me.

"I know," I took in a deep breath and let it out slowly as I allowed Kyle's embrace to comfort my wounded soul. "But my dad came to the mortuary with us. As I knew he would, he took charge and made all the decisions needing to be made. I'm afraid poor Helen is pretty broken, and Jenna is so exhausted from taking care of her mother that she looks like she is on the verge of collapse. I would have welcomed your support, but it is more important to me that you do whatever you need to do to get out of here."

"I really don't know why Hunter wanted me to stay until today. I feel fine." Kyle let out a sharp breath as he adjusted his position. "Well maybe not fine but I certainly don't need to be here."

"Hunter is just being careful," I said. "And I for one am glad he wants to make sure you're ready to leave the hospital before you do." My chest tightened. "I don't know what I would have done if I'd lost you too."

Kyle turned his head and kissed my forehead. "I know you

are concerned about me and I don't want you to worry. I can't even begin to imagine how I would feel if you hadn't somehow managed to escape the explosion with no more than a bruise on your leg and a bump on your head. It really is a miracle that a beam landed on top of you, and you got out of it without even one broken bone."

I shrugged. "I may be tiny, but I'm tough. Titanium tough, according to Hunter."

"And I am grateful for that. I know this has been hard on you, so I want to assure you that I am being an exemplary patient and doing everything Hunter recommends no matter how tedious I may find it."

I kissed Kyle gently on the lips. "Thank you. I appreciate that. Did you hear about the tests? Will I be able to spring you this afternoon?"

"I asked the nurse, but all she would tell me was that Hunter would be in to speak to me once he got out of surgery."

I settled in next to Kyle's warmth. I listened to his heartbeat beneath my head, which, in an odd way, seemed to calm my jagged nerves. "As happy as I am that Hunter is being overly cautious when it comes to your health, I will be happy to get you home where I can take care of you myself. Not that I'm a great nurse mind you, but I've missed you. I want to have you close at hand so I can keep an eye on you and assure myself that everything is going to be okay."

Kyle squeezed the hand he held. "I've missed you too, and I may literally go insane if I can't get home to my computer and start trying to figure out who did this terrible thing. I've been thinking about it a lot, and there just doesn't seem to be any obvious suspects."

"Have you talked to Roy?" I referred to Deputy Roy Fisher.

Kyle nodded. "More than once, and all he can really say is that he is stumped. I know he has spoken to everyone who might have been in a position to see something, but so far, no one claims to have witnessed anything suspicious. At this point, he doesn't have a clue as to who might have blown up the building or why."

"I'm sure Roy is doing everything he knows to do, and I know we should just let him do his job, but there is no way I am letting Lloyd and Harriet's killer get away with this."

"I agree. As soon as I can get out of here, I'll start digging for the answers we need."

I gently moved my hand over Kyle's chest, giving thanks for the fact that he hadn't been more seriously hurt. If we hadn't been late to the meeting... Well, I didn't want to think about that. "Grandpa and Doc want to come by once we get home. I think they need to be part of things. They both seem so lost. It is going to be even worse if Bookman doesn't make it. I feel so bad for them, but really don't know how to help them through this."

"They lost a friend and an acquaintance and may still lose others. From what I understand, Bookman and Hank are both in critical condition. I overheard a nurse say that at this point, their recovery is far from guaranteed."

"I heard that, as well. I just feel so bad for everyone. I feel like I should be doing more, but honestly, I have no idea what to do."

Kyle used a forefinger to tuck a lock of my long curly hair that had fallen across my face behind my ear. "There really isn't anything you can do except let them know you are there for them, and of course, we will make sure they know they are part of the team."

I let out a breath as I tried to find a way to let go of some of the tension I'd been carrying. I knew that finding answers that would help me to make sense of this horrible event was the only thing that was going to keep me sane. "Kate is going to have a coronary once she finds out we are nosing around."

Kyle shrugged. "Honestly, I don't care what Deputy Kate Baldwin thinks about our involvement. I know she is Roy's partner, I know she does not believe that civilians should be involved in police investigations regardless of their success in solving past crimes, and I know she can make things difficult for Roy, so I have tried to tread lightly in the past, but this is personal."

I smiled and cuddled in a bit closer, which caused Kyle to flinch. "Sorry."

Kyle tightened his arm around me as I tried to move away just a bit. "So, how is Helen holding up?" Kyle asked. "She has been on my mind all day."

"She is somehow getting through it. If I had to guess, she is just taking things one moment at a time. If Bookman wakes up, that will make it easier, although she will still have to deal with the loss of a lifelong friend."

"Helen and Harriet have been close friends for a very long time."

"Since before I was born. I'm not sure exactly when she moved to Paradise Lake, but I can't remember a time when she wasn't here. The fact that she is no longer going to be found sitting at the secretary's desk just outside the mayor's office on any given weekday is going to be very odd indeed."

"Of course, there is no longer a secretary's desk or a mayor's office," Kyle pointed out.

"I suppose that is true." I looked up when I heard Hunter come into the room. His smile turned to a frown, I suspect as a reaction to seeing me cuddled up with Kyle. I knew that our being together was weird for him, so I slowly slipped off the bed. Hunter didn't say anything, and I didn't either, but the tension in the room couldn't be denied.

"So, am I getting out of here?" Kyle asked in a voice that seemed just a tad bit too cheery given the situation.

Hunter glanced at the report in his hand. "You are. Everything looks good. I guess I don't need to tell you to take it easy for a while. No lifting or strenuous activity of any sort. I am going to want to see you in a week so we can take another look at those ribs, but it appears you are good to go. I'll tell the nurse to start your paperwork." Then Hunter turned his attention toward me. "And how are you feeling? Any dizziness or nausea?"

I smiled and shook my head. "My leg is a little tender, but otherwise I am feeling perfectly fine thanks to you."

"To be honest, you were lucky. It would have been so much worse if that beam had fallen just an inch or two one way or another." Hunter looked back toward Kyle. "I'm going to have the nurse go over the discharge instructions which I expect to be followed to a tee."

"I'll do whatever you ask. And thank you. For everything."

Hunter shrugged. "Just doing my job." He nodded at me and then turned to leave.

"Do you think he is ever going to get used to seeing us together?" I asked Kyle after Hunter exited the room.

"The two of you were together for a long time, and we have only been together for a few months. Give him time. Eventually, I'm sure things won't be so awkward."

"Yeah. I guess. I brought you a change of clothes. I'm going to run out to the car and get them while the nurse gets your paperwork ready. I won't be long." I ran toward the elevator just as the door began to close. I slipped in to find Hunter already inside.

"Going down?" he asked.

I nodded. "I'm sorry about the bed thing. I wasn't thinking."

"It's okay," Hunter said as the elevator started down toward the lobby. "I know the past couple of days have been stressful, and I know you've been worried about Kyle. How did Helen do today?"

"Okay," I answered. "Dad was there, and he took care of everything."

"Your dad is a good man. I've always liked and admired him. I miss our talks."

"And he misses chatting with you as well. The girls miss you too," I referred to my sisters, Ashley and Gracie. "It would be okay if you wanted to come around sometimes."

Hunter hesitated.

"We did it before. Dated and then settled into a friendship. We can do it again. I know that this time is different with Kyle and all, but I'm not ready to not have you in my life."

Hunter's expression grew serious. "I know. I will admit that seeing you with Kyle is tough, although I do actually like the guy and consider him a friend, which makes it both harder and easier to know that he now has what I once had."

I felt my heart squeeze just a bit. Hunter had been in my life for a long time. I couldn't bear it if he didn't continue to be in my life in some capacity. "I'm sorry that my being with Kyle is hard for you. I can understand why it might be. But we did talk about our relationship and decided that what we had was wrong for both of us long before Kyle and I got together."

Hunter let out a breath. "I know. And I remember that I am the one who actually started dating first, and I remember that it was hard for you as well. We've been friends for a long time. It is important to me that we are able to remain friends in the future. I'll text you sometime. Maybe I can take the girls to a movie or your dad for a drink."

"They'd like that."

We exited the elevator at the lobby. I continued on toward the front door, and Hunter continued down the hall. Love and friendship. The best life had to offer, but more often than not, the most complicated as well.

# CHAPTER 3

I called Grandpa once Kyle and I made it back to his house. He informed me that he and Doc would be right over. I knew in my mind that Kyle should probably rest for a few days before tackling the latest deaths in Serenity but it had been two days since the explosion, and I knew that most everyone in the community was on edge waiting for the bomber to be caught. Kyle and I had always worked well with Roy, although things had become tricky since his new partner had come to town. Still, given the importance of the investigation, we'd decided to invite him to meet with us as well.

"Any updates to the situation?" I asked Roy once we'd all assembled.

"Not really. The crime scene unit has determined a bomb and not something like a gas leak caused the explosion. The blast originated from the south side of the building near where Harriet and Lloyd were sitting. We don't know how the bomb came to be in the building or why no one seemed to have noticed it prior to the explosion. Kate and I have canvassed the area surrounding the town offices and have spoken to every individual who might have seen something. So far, we haven't found a single person who noticed anyone loitering with a backpack. We've checked with the USPS as well as FedEx, DHL, and UPS, and none claim to have delivered a package to the town offices in over a week. At this point, we are operating under the assumption that the bomb was brought to the building by an individual who either dropped off a package or broke into the town offices and planted the bomb which was set to go off either remotely or on a timer."

"The crime scene guys don't know which?" I asked.

"Not yet. They are working on it, but there was so much damage to the building that they haven't been able to access much of the rubble. We'll know more once they are able to stabilize or tear down the remaining walls and the team can get in and do a thorough search. I know you both had just arrived when the bomb went off and wouldn't have had time to see anything. I spoke to Jeff who didn't remember seeing a box or backpack, but I am hoping that either Bookman or Hank might remember seeing something if they wake up."

"When they wake up," Grandpa corrected.

Roy nodded. "Yes, when they wake up."

"So what have you come up with in terms of motive?" I asked. "Are you thinking that the council as a whole was the target or that one of the individuals on the council was the target and the others were just collateral damage?"

"I wish I knew. At this point, I don't even know where to start in terms of a suspect list." Roy looked at Kyle. "Tuesday wasn't a regular council night. Why were you all there, anyway?"

"Tj and I were out trick or treating with the kids when I received a text from Harriet that an emergency meeting had been called. The text sounded urgent, so we handed the kids off to Jenna and headed over."

Roy frowned. "Was it normally Harriet who called these extra meetings?"

Kyle nodded. "If any of the council members wanted to schedule a closed-door meeting and it wasn't urgent, they would tell Harriet, and she would set a date and time and notify everyone well in advance, usually via email. If a council member had an urgent request and a meeting was needed right away, then Harriet would usually call or text everyone."

"And are these secret meetings part of the town's bylaws?" Roy asked.

"Yes, and no," Kyle answered. "There is a provision in the bylaws for the council to meet behind closed doors. This provision, I believe, was included to provide a way for the council to deal with situations that were sensitive and confidential, and therefore not appropriate for a public forum. Prior to Mayor Harper's death, I only remember attending two closed-door meetings in the two years I have been on the council. Since Harper's death, it seems to me that these closed-door meetings have become the norm. Personally, I have a problem with the fact that so much of the town council's business is being conducted behind closed doors. I have spoken to the other town council members about it on several occasions. Bookman tended to side with me, but both Hank and Lloyd felt that our discussions relating to several sensitive issues currently being looked at by the council were too controversial to be debated in an open forum."

"And Jeff?" Roy asked.

"He is new to the council, having taken one of the two empty seats. I don't think he felt comfortable choosing sides until he knew more about it."

"So Harriet called this last minute on Tuesday, and during that meeting, a bomb went off killing the two people closest to the bomb including Harriet. If the meeting was called on the fly, how did the bomber even know that the council was going to be in the building when it exploded?" Doc wondered.

"Good question," I said.

"I suppose that the bomber might have been the individual behind the emergency meeting," Kyle suggested.

"So you think the bomber might have created a situation

where an emergency meeting would be called, and then planted the bomb to go off once everyone arrived?" I asked. "It seems unlikely. If you stop to think about it, the likelihood of the person who planted the bomb being able to anticipate the timing of the council members arriving would be close to impossible."

Kyle shrugged. "It does seem unlikely, although I suppose it could have happened that way. At this point, there is no way to know for sure one way or the other."

Grandpa leaned forward onto his forearms. His expression grew thoughtful. "If the last-minute meeting hadn't been called, would the building have been empty when the bomb went off?"

Kyle nodded. "The town offices close at five. The bomb went off around six."

"What if the bomber didn't intend for there to be human casualties?" Grandpa asked.

Doc furrowed his brows in an expression that seemed to convey confusion. "Why would anyone blow up an empty building?"

"Maybe someone wanted to destroy something within the building, such as contracts, minutes of past town council meetings, copies of notes or other documents," Grandpa replied.

"Isn't everything in the cloud these days?" I asked.

"Everything current is, but not everything from the past has been entered," Kyle answered. "In fact, getting the archives uploaded into the cloud is one of the projects I've been meaning to get to but somehow never found the time to deal with."

"So the target could have been any of the six people who would be expected to attend the meeting, the town council as a whole, or the building and its contents," Roy concluded. "It's going to be hard to know which to focus on. I guess all we can do is systematically look at every possible angle and eliminate scenarios that don't fit the evidence."

"Where do we even start?" I groaned, as the fatigue of the past two days sucked the last of the energy from my body. At this point, the task in front of us looked to be insurmountable.

Roy looked at Kyle. "What had the group gathered to discuss on the night of the bombing?"

Kyle narrowed his gaze and slowly shook his head. "I don't really know. The text I received was vague and only said that my presence was required at the town hall. The text didn't explain why the meeting had been called, but we've had a number of emergency meetings lately, so I wasn't all that surprised by the request." Kyle furrowed his brow as if trying to remember. "I hadn't been part of the discussion prior to the building coming down since I was late to the meeting. I suppose Jeff might know."

"I'll ask him. In the meantime, what would you say are the hot topics the council has been dealing with as of late?"

Kyle leaned back in his chair. He momentarily closed his eyes and lifted his arms over his head in a move that made it appear as if he was trying both stretch out his sore muscles and center his jumbled thoughts. I felt so bad for him. Not only was he physically injured, but I knew that the enormity of trying to put the town back together had fallen on his shoulders. I really wasn't sure how one person was supposed to deal with such a huge task, but I knew that if anyone could, it would be Kyle.

"I suppose the number one hot topic in the past few months has been finding a full-time mayor," Kyle eventually answered Roy's question. "Bookman agreed to fill in temporarily after Mayor Harper died, but he made it clear since day one that he has no desire to take on the job permanently, and he has been very vocal about the fact that his willingness to assume the role is approaching an end."

"So what's the holdup with appointing someone?" Roy asked.

"The bylaws state that the mayor will be appointed by the town council and that a minimum of five of the six town council members must agree on the individual appointed. At this point, we only have five town council members, but there has been a general agreement that if four of the five agree, we can move forward."

"And you can't find a candidate that four of the five can agree on?" Roy asked.

Kyle shook his head. "This is new territory for everyone involved. Mayor Wallaby was the acting mayor for more than two decades, so the need to appoint a new mayor never really came up. After he resigned, there was a bit of discussion, but Judge Harper seemed like an obvious choice, so there was actually very little debate about the matter. Now, however, there doesn't seem to be a clear option. If Bookman wanted to do it long term, I think everyone would have gotten behind him, which would mean that the council would only be tasked with finding an additional council member to replace him, but he has made it clear that he is much too busy to take on the full-time position. None of the other town council members are interested in the job, which means that we are looking for an appointment from outside the group. In a way, I think it could be a good thing to bring in some fresh blood and a new perspective, but it seems as if everyone has their own idea as to who should be considered for the job and so far, we as a group, have been unable to reach a consensus. In fact, we are so completely divided that I am beginning to wonder if we'll ever find a candidate the group as a whole approves of."

"What about changing things up so that rather than the town council appointing the mayor, an election is held and the residents are given a voice?" Doc queried.

"That has been suggested as well, but in order to change the bylaws to allow for the mayor to be elected rather than appointed, the council would have to vote to do so, and, at this point, there hasn't been consensus on that either."

I knew that Kyle had been feeling some pressure to take on the position, but he'd made it clear that while he was happy to serve on the town council, running the town was not how he wanted to spend the majority of his day.

"Okay, moving on from the appointment of a new mayor, what other sorts of items has the council been dealing with that might be considered to be hot topic items?" Roy asked.

"James Kingston has been creating a lot of grief for the council," Kyle answered after considering the question for a moment.

James was a real estate developer and one of the richest men in the area.

"James has bought up so much property in the past two decades that I suspect he collects it the same way my mom used to collect Franklin Mint Collectible plates," Roy added. "I seem to recall he turned most of that property into vacation rentals."

"He has. Unfortunately for the council, one of the main things on Bookman's agenda during his brief tenure as mayor has been to pass a bill which would outlaw the use of single-family homes as vacation rentals within the town limits. The debate has always been a volatile one. On one side of the argument are the men and women who bought up single-family homes and then turned around and made a lot of money renting them to both families and groups who wanted an alternative to commercial lodging properties. On the other side of the argument are the residents who don't want to deal with the noise often associated with a vacation property, as well as the owners of the existing lodging properties who see the vacation rentals as a new source of competition. James Kingston has made a lot of money from his rental properties, so it was not surprising that he would clash with the interim mayor, who firmly believes that vacation rentals and the noise and the increase in the crime rate that come with them should not be allowed in neighborhoods where families who work and raise their children live."

"Do you think that James would blow up the entire town council over this issue?" Roy asked Kyle.

"Honestly, no, but there is a lot of money on the table so I suppose the issue, in general, could have caused someone involved to go over the edge."

Roy jotted down James's name. "Anyone else?"

Kyle dug his forefingers into his temple. I suspected that the headache he'd been dealing with since the explosion was back. Hunter had given Kyle pain medication for those times when the pain was at its worst, but as far as I could tell, Kyle had declined to take it.

"I don't know who else might have a motive," Kyle eventually answered. "If I stop to really think about it, I'm sure I can come up with a short list. It's so hard to know what will set someone off. As angry as James seemed to be when he realized that the acting mayor wanted to change a law which would end up costing him millions of dollars over time, I think that Elsa Winter was even angrier over the issue relating to her dog."

"Dog?" Doc asked.

"Elsa Winter's dog keeps getting out of her yard in spite of the fact that she has gone to quite a lot of trouble to keep him inside," Kyle explained. "The dog is not only clever and determined, but he is also aggressive and unruly and is basically terrorizing the neighborhood. The neighbors living closest to Elsa got together and signed a petition which would require Elsa to either get rid of the dog or move. When the petition was presented to the council, their approach to the situation was divided, which seemed to anger everyone. Bookman told me later that one of the more vocal neighbors threatened to kill the dog if it wasn't dealt with."

"That seems overly drastic," I pointed out.

"I don't disagree," Kyle said. "I'm just using the situation to make the point that, as far as I could tell, Elsa was just as angry about her dog, as James was about the money he would lose if the law was changed. When gauging who might funnel their anger into an act of violence and who might not, I'm not sure you can measure the potential for violence based on the dollar value of what is perceived to be lost."

I shrugged. "That makes sense. I'm sure Elsa values her dog even more than James values his money."

Roy groaned and put his little notepad in his pocket. "I can see this isn't going to be easy. Let's just all make a list of whoever comes to mind and then take it from there."

After Roy, Doc, and Grandpa left, I wandered into the kitchen to dig up some dinner for Kyle and me. My dad and his fiancée, town veterinarian, Rosalie Tyler, had agreed to keep an eye on my sisters, Ashley and Gracie, for a few days so that I could stay with Kyle and help him out should he require any help as his ribs healed and his strength returned.

"I think we might need to order a pizza," I said to Kyle after taking an inventory of his meager supplies.

"Pizza is fine. In fact, after eating hospital food for two days, pizza sounds pretty darn good. I could use some fresh air. Let's just head over to Rob's and eat there."

"Sounds good to me." Rob's Pizza was a comfy joint with vinyl booths, red-checkered tablecloths, team pictures on the walls, video games, and the best pizza west of the Rockies. I loved coming to Rob's. Besides the fact that he made the best pizza around, Rob provided a cozy atmosphere, with a lived-in, hometown feel.

"I think this is just what I need," Kyle said as we slid into a booth in the back.

I looked around the room which had been decorated in anticipation of the upcoming holiday. "It looks like Rob has already traded out his Halloween decorations for garland and white lights."

"I guess it is November."

"I can't believe it will be Thanksgiving in a few weeks. I guess that even under normal circumstances, once Halloween arrives, it seems like it is a mad dash toward Christmas."

"Speaking of Thanksgiving," Kyle said, "I wanted to ask what you think about throwing a big dinner at my place? It will be our first major holiday as a couple, and I want it to be special."

I hesitated before I answered. "While I do love that idea, the resort is closed over the Thanksgiving holiday, so we usually have a huge dinner out at Maggie's Hideaway. I don't think Dad would mind passing off hosting duties if you really want to do it, but we usually invite a good thirty people. Sometimes more. Everyone pitches in buffet style, which makes it doable."

"If we move the furniture, we'd be able to seat thirty at my place," Kyle pointed out.

"That's true. If you want to host, I'll talk to my dad about it. Will your mom be joining us this year or will she be heading to your uncle's like she did last year?"

"She'll be in town. She usually tries to trade off to keep everyone happy."

I took a sip of the wine the waitress had just dropped off. "It would be fun to have the holiday at the house I still associate with Zachary. You know he actually tried to make a turkey for the two of us one year. He planned to serve it for lunch the day before Thanksgiving, but he ended up burning it, so we had canned chili. He was really upset that his plans didn't work out, but as far as I'm concerned, it was still a very memorable lunch. He set the table and even used a tablecloth, which I'd never seen him use prior to that lunch or at any point after. The meal itself might not have worked out the way he hoped, but it meant a lot to me that he tried." I smiled at the memory. "Did I mention that I spoke to Zachary on the night of the explosion?"

Kyle raised a brow. "Spoke to him?"

"He was there in my head when I was unconscious. We played a game of chess and had a good chat."

Kyle put his hand over mine. "I guess that isn't surprising. The two of you had a special relationship. It makes sense that your subconscious might seek him out during such a traumatic event."

I smiled. "I really do miss him. Sometimes I find myself daydreaming about playing chess with him with that handmade set he had in the basement. The one with the little drawer and the chip in the corner. Do you still have it?"

"When I remodeled the house, I cleared out the basement, but I seem to remember the chess set ended up in the attic. We can look for it when we get back. Are you are staying over tonight?"

I nodded. "Dad and Rosalie are going to keep an eye on Ashley and Gracie for a few days so I can be available to nurse you back to health. I would like to stop by the resort to pick up Echo and Trooper on the way back to your place." Echo was my dog, and Trooper was Kyle's.

"I like that plan. And I want to thank your dad for picking Trooper up and bringing him out to the resort on Tuesday. The poor guy would have freaked out if no one had shown up to let him out."

"Dad was happy to help out. Trooper is part of the family." The conversation paused as the pizza was delivered to our table. Talk about cheesy perfection. While the food was to die for I, couldn't get the explosion and the subsequent loss of life out of my mind. "I've been thinking about the fact that Lloyd was the town council member closest to the bomb. If the bomb had been placed to eliminate one of the individuals in the room, it seems likely in my mind that the bomb was intended for him. He's a controversial guy who not only wields a lot of power but has as many enemies as supporters."

Kyle took a bite of his pizza then set it down and took a sip of his water. "It is true that of all the council members, his appointment was the most controversial." Kyle drummed his fingers on the table. "As a developer, he has angered a lot of folks who want Serenity to keep its small-town feel. Yet he does have supporters amongst those who have benefited from the jobs his developments have created. I'm sure we could come up with a long list of people who hold a grudge against the guy, but I suppose the real question is: would any of those with a grudge actually kill him in such a violent manner?"

I had to agree with Kyle that if any of the town council members had been the target, then the method of elimination had been drastically over the top. "Maybe the bomb wasn't about a single person. Maybe someone simply wanted to make a statement and wasn't worried about collateral damage. As crazy as it seems, there are people out there who are simply after the rush."

"If that is true, it is going to be next to impossible to figure out who did this."

"Yeah," I groaned. "A random act of violence would most definitely complicate things."

# CHAPTER 4

Friday, November 3

"You're up early," Kyle said when he joined me in the kitchen the next morning.

I glanced out the window to see that the rain showers of yesterday had given way to snow showers today. "I had a weird dream and couldn't get back to sleep, so I got up."

Kyle poured himself a cup of coffee and sat down at the table with me. "Do you want to talk about your dream?"

I turned slightly. "I dreamt about Zachary. He's been on my mind more than usual since he is the one I imagined when I was unconscious, and then we talked about him last night. His appearance in my dream is most likely the result of remembering things I haven't thought about in years, but it felt so real; not at all like a dream."

"Do you remember the content of the dream?"

I sat back and tried to pull the dream into my consciousness. "It's pretty fuzzy, but I do remember that Zachary and I were playing chess just like we had when I was unconscious."

"So do you think that your subconscious mind is using these dreams to tell you something?"

I shrugged. "I'm not really sure. I suppose these visions of Zachary could just be my mind trying to make sense of everything that has happened. I know Zachary is dead and that he isn't actually speaking to me, but I can't seem to get him out of my mind. Maybe I just miss him. Maybe playing chess with him represents a simpler time. Maybe deep down, I know something that might be relevant to the case. Maybe Zachary's presence is simply my subconscious trying to remind me of what it is I need to remember."

"You asked about the chess set that used to be in the basement. We never did look for it last night. We can look now if you want."

I shook my head as I poured a second cup of coffee. "I'd like to find the chess set, but it can wait. We talked about the idea that Lloyd might have been the target of the bombing last night, but we got sidetracked talking about a random act of violence. While possible, I really don't think a random act of violence is what is going on."

"I agree. We did let ourselves get sidetracked. I spoke to Jeff, and he said that while he didn't know why the emergency meeting had been called, based on what was said after he arrived, he had the impression that Lloyd was the one to call it. If you add to that the fact that Lloyd was the council member sitting closest to the bomb and that he is undeniably the most controversial councilman, I think taking a closer look at his business dealings might be a good idea."

"Why would Lloyd call a meeting and then blow himself up?"

"I'm not saying that is what happened, but the more I think about things, if there was a single member of the council who angered someone enough to blow up an entire building, it would be Lloyd. If it turns out his business dealings were not the cause, so much the better, but we really have nothing at this point and looking into his current projects seems like as good a place as any to start."

"Okay, so what do you want to do?"

"Let's see if we can get into his house and his office and take a look around. It would make sense that someone would have confiscated his computer by now, but if not, we'll take that as well. I'm sure his phone was on him and is most likely in a million pieces by this point. I can pull his phone records to see who he spoke to on the day of the blast."

"Should we call Roy?"

Kyle nodded. "I'll call him to let him know what we are doing. If he has a concern about our plan, he can let us know."

"Okay. I'm going to run upstairs and jump in the shower. Maybe we can grab something to eat while we're out." I turned and headed toward the stairway. I paused and turned back. "I wonder what happened to Lloyd's car. I wonder what happened to everyone's car."

"Mine was in my driveway when we arrived home from the hospital. I guess someone, maybe Roy, might have had it towed over."

"So maybe the other cars in the lot were towed to the homes of their owners as well. We'll look for Lloyd's when we check out his house. I'm not sure that locating the vehicles which had been parked in the lot is even important, but maybe one of the vehicles can provide a clue."

Kyle was on the phone with Roy when I arrived back downstairs. The men seemed to be discussing permits of some sort, so I headed into the other room to check in with Ashley and Gracie. I knew they'd been terrified when they'd learned about the explosion and the fact that Kyle and I had both been taken to the hospital. I could understand their fear. Our mother had been taken to a hospital four and a half years ago and never came back. When I'd learned that I'd been assigned as their guardian,

I was even more terrified than they were, but somehow we'd gotten through the crisis and become a family.

"Hey, Gracie, I'm just checking in. How is everything?"

"Everything is good. Cuervo and Snowball got into a fight, but Papa broke it up. He said that Cuervo is missing you. I'm missing you too. When will you be home?"

"In a day or two." Cuervo was my angsty orange tabby who most definitely was not a fan of change. "Is Snowball okay?"

"She's fine. Papa is going to have Cuervo sleep with him and Rosalie since you and Echo are both gone."

"That sounds like a good idea. Cuervo hates to sleep alone, especially when it is cold."

"You got a package today."

"A package?" Suddenly, all I could think about was another bomb. "What sort of package?"

"I don't know. A man brought it to the house."

"Does Papa know about the package?"

"No, he is over at the stables with Rosalie checking on the new baby colts. The man who brought the package just left it on the porch, but it's snowing, so I brought it in."

"Is Grandpa there?" I could feel the panic begin to build. Since we lived at a resort, we had a lot of deliveries, so normally receiving a package was a yawn-worthy event, but with everything that had happened this week, I didn't want to take any chances.

"Grandpa is in the den. He is watching a movie."

"Can you put him on the phone, please?"

"Okay. Hang on."

I listened as Gracie ran down the stairs and across the living room floor. In my mind, I couldn't help but imagine the innocent looking package blowing up. I held my breath as I waited and listened for the sound of a loud bang. Less than a minute after Gracie went to find him, Grandpa came on the line.

I explained about the package and suggested that he might want to check it. I told him to be careful, and he said he would. He continued to talk to me as he headed toward the entry where Gracie had left the box sitting on the table.

"I see it. Hang on while I get my knife to cut the tape."

"Be careful," I said again. "It's probably just something I ordered and forgot about but given what's happened..."

"I know. Hang on."

"It's a box full of cash," he said a few seconds later.

"Cash? How much cash?"

"I'm not sure. If you want to hang on, I can count it, but it looks like at least several thousand dollars."

"Is there a note?"

Grandpa took a moment before he answered. I supposed he was looking through the box. "No. Nothing is in the box other than the cash."

"Okay, I'm going to have Roy come by and pick it up. I don't know what is going on, but having someone send a box of cash to me is definitely suspicious. Given everything else that is going on, Roy will want to look for prints and other physical evidence. Given the timing, the cash is very likely to be related to the destruction of the town hall in some way."

"Related how?"

"I have no idea, but it isn't every day that one receives a box of cash. I think that until this bombing case is wrapped up, we should tell both Ashley and Gracie not to accept the delivery of any packages, or to bring any packages left on the porch inside unless they check with an adult first."

"Yeah, that's probably a good idea. I'll put the box up until Roy gets here. How's Kyle doing today?"

"He seems to be hanging in there. I can tell his ribs hurt, but he never complains. He's talking to Roy right now, and then we are going to head over and check out Lloyd's place."

"Do you have new evidence to suggest that he was the target?"

"No. But Jeff told Kyle that he was pretty sure it was Lloyd who'd called the meeting, he was the closest to the blast, and he was the most controversial council member. If there is a scandal to uncover, chances are that it will link back to him."

After I hung up with Grandpa, I went in search of Kyle, who was just hanging up with Roy. I stopped him and asked him to let me speak to Roy. After I told Roy about the cash, he agreed to head to the resort and pick up it up. Five minutes after he hung up with me, he called me back to let me know that a box had been delivered to Jeff in his hospital room, which had also contained a lot of cash.

"What on earth is going on?" I asked Kyle, as he grabbed a few tools he thought he might need to break into Lloyd's place.

"I don't know, but I don't like it. I wonder if anyone else received cash."

"Roy didn't mention anyone else, but I suppose that others could have boxes waiting for them that they haven't discovered yet. The fact that both Jeff and I received the cash makes me feel like the deliveries are linked to the explosion. Of course, if that were true, then you and Bookman would receive packages as well. I know you haven't, but I wonder if he has."

"Call Helen and ask her."

I called Helen while Kyle drove us to Lloyd's. She confirmed that they hadn't received any packages, but said that she'd keep an eye out. Talk about a crazy twist to this crazy story. When we arrived at Lloyd's place, I couldn't help but gasp. His residence was really more of an estate, and what an estate it was. Lloyd had been a developer in the area for a lot of years, and during his career, he'd managed to rake in a lot of money. The three-story home he'd built on the eastern shore of Paradise Lake had been featured in both Architectural Digest and Lakefront Living.

Kyle and I didn't have a key or an alarm code, which would have allowed us to access the home, but the estate was pretty isolated, so surprisingly, Kyle, who'd never been in favor of breaking and entering during past investigations, suggested we take a chance and break in. I kept an eye on the front drive while Kyle found the power source to the house and disabled it, thereby disabling the security system. He then jimmied the lock on the garage door. Once inside, Kyle was able to verify that the generator was not tied into the security system, so he used tools we found in Lloyd's well-stocked tool room to break into the house through the back door.

"Wow, this place is gorgeous," I said, as I walked through the house to the back where a wall of windows looked out over the lake. The house was situated on the property to provide a view of either the mountains or the water from pretty much every window.

"Lloyd was very creative with the design, and while in any other circumstance I might take my time and look around, today I just want to find his office and get out of here. Let's split up." Kyle suggested. "You look on this floor, and I'll head upstairs. If you find what we are looking for, give a holler, and I'll do the same."

The bottom floor of the home was laid out for entertaining. The entry opened into a great room that, based its size, would have held a hundred guests. The huge gourmet kitchen was separated from the great room by a long counter lined with barstools, and beyond the kitchen was a game room with a pool table and video games. Lloyd was single. As far as I knew, he'd never married nor had children. I had to wonder why he'd wanted such a huge home. I knew there were at least five bedrooms and eight baths, so maybe he used his residence to entertain clients.

"The office is up here," Kyle called down from upstairs after he'd been searching for a few minutes.

I abandoned my tour and headed toward the staircase. The office, like every other room in the home, was huge. It not only featured a floor to ceiling fireplace, but two of the walls were lined with floor to ceiling bookshelves.

Kyle headed directly to Lloyd's desk. He'd brought an empty box with him, so rather than looking at every item on the desk and in the drawers, he simply began filling up the box. Once the desk had been emptied, he turned to the file cabinets, but they were locked. Kyle tried the keys on a keyring he had found, but none of them unlocked the cabinets.

"We'll start with this," Kyle said, scooping up a stack of files from a tall table behind the desk. "Do you see his laptop?"

"No, but to be honest, I would have thought he'd have a desktop computer in his home office."

"We'll probably find his desktop in his office in town. He may have had his laptop with him. Let's start with what we've found. If we feel like we have cause, we can come back and break into the file cabinets."

"Are we going to break into his office in town?"

Kyle held up the keyring he'd been using to attempt to open the file cabinets. "I'm hoping one of these opens the office, and we won't have to break in."

"It is probably alarmed."

"Maybe, but we may find a way around that. If not, we'll come up with plan B."

We tried to get into the office, but the keys we had didn't work and, unlike the estate, it was located in a public place with a lot of auto and pedestrian traffic. We couldn't cut the power as we had at Lloyd's home, so we took the items we'd recovered from this home office, and headed back to Kyle's house. Kyle called Roy, and he confirmed that Lloyd's car had been towed to the impound lot. He didn't know if the crime scene unit had gone through it yet, but said that he would find out and then he'd get back to us. While Kyle had been on the line with Roy, he'd asked if law enforcement personnel had searched Lloyd's office. Roy answered that Kate had been gathering information relating to each of the victims while he had been working with the crime scene unit in an attempt to nail down the specifics of the blast. She hadn't come into work yet that day, but when she did, he'd ask her for an update.

# CHAPTER 5

"So did we find a smoking gun?" I asked after Kyle had taken everything from the box and laid it out on the long dining table.

"I'm not sure if I found a smoking gun, but I may have found something," Kyle said. "According to a notepad Lloyd had left on his desk, it looks like he had a meeting with James Kingston on Tuesday afternoon." Kyle paused and then continued. "I guess it makes sense that Kingston might have reached out to Lloyd. As a developer, Lloyd has tended to support investors in the area. He is usually pro anything that is real estate related. Maybe James met with Lloyd to try to come up with a strategy to suppress the movement to ban the vacation rentals."

"So does that make James even more of a suspect than he already was?"

Kyle tilted his head slightly. "Not really. Chances are that Lloyd sided with James regarding the ban on vacation rentals, so James would have no motivation to kill him. I guess I'll just pass this information on to Roy. If he feels it warrants further investigation, he can talk to James."

"Makes sense. Anything else?"

Kyle looked at his computer. "I pulled up Lloyd's phone records. He received a series of calls from a burner phone in the three-day period leading up to the bombing. The first call from this particular number showed up on Sunday. There were five other calls from the same number on Sunday, seven on Monday, and four on Tuesday. The last call Lloyd received from this number came in just an hour before we received the text that an emergency meeting had been called."

I leaned forward and rested my arms on the table in front of me. "That seems like it might be a promising lead. Has the number shown up before?"

Kyle shook his head. "I went back into Lloyd's cell records for three months, and the first time the number showed up was Sunday. Given the fact that I traced the number back to a burner phone, I'm not sure that is going to help us, but I'm going to do some poking around and see if I can find any additional information relating to the calls. If the calls originated from a consistent location, like a home or office, I might be able to figure out where they were made."

"At this point, it really does look like Lloyd and/or James might have been involved in whatever occurred, although it seems as if there are a lot of holes in every theory we have come up with."

"I have to agree with that. Lloyd did die as a result of the blast. If he was involved in any way, then it seems obvious that something went very wrong. By the way," Kyle added. "Roy picked up the money that was sent to the resort. The amount of cash inside was exactly six thousand dollars. Does that amount mean anything to you?"

I shook my head. "No. Not off hand. Did Jeff get the same amount?"

"Jeff received fourteen thousand, seven hundred dollars."

"That seems oddly specific."

"Jeff said that his healthcare insurance deductible is fourteen thousand dollars and that he has a separate deductible for prescriptions, which he thinks might come out to around seven hundred dollars."

My eyes grew wide. "My out-of-pocket deductible is six thousand dollars. I haven't even stopped to think about the fact that my time in the hospital was going to cost me some of my hard-earned savings. I'm pretty sure I haven't received a bill yet."

"Jeff hasn't either. He doesn't know who the cash was from, but he was thrilled to have his deductible covered."

"Okay, so someone has decided to pay our deductibles. Do you think it is the bomber?"

Kyle frowned. "It seems unlikely, but I suppose it is possible, especially if the bomb was not meant to harm innocent bystanders. I suppose the cash could have been sent by a Good Samaritan."

"It seems as if a Good Samaritan would simply make a donation on our behalf directly to the hospital."

"That is probably true."

"So did anyone other than Jeff and I receive cash?"

Kyle shook his head. "Not as of this point. Roy and I discussed it and decided that whoever sent the cash sent it based on need. Hank, Bookman, and I have a lot of money. Paying our hospital bill won't cause hardship for any of us. You and Jeff, on the other hand, don't currently enjoy the same level of financial comfort."

I supposed that made sense. The fact that someone sent me the cash I would need to cover the hospital bill I hadn't even stopped to worry about was nice, but not knowing who sent it was a little creepy.

"Okay, say this theory is true. How did the person who sent the cash know how much our hospital bills were going to be? As I've already said, I haven't received a statement from the hospital yet. I doubt I will receive one until the end of the month."

"I'm not sure how the person who sent the cash got this

information. Roy wasn't certain either. It appears as if someone might have hacked into the hospital's financial records and looked up your deductible."

I didn't like the sound of that. "Did Roy say anything else?"

"He has Lloyd's laptop. I guess the guys at the impound lot found it in the trunk of his car. The laptop is password protected, so Roy is going to drop it by my place this evening after he gets off. He figures that while the county's tech guys will eventually get in, I'll get in quicker."

"I imagine that he is right about that. In the meantime, maybe you should take a break." I couldn't help but notice how completely exhausted Kyle looked. He'd only been out of the hospital for a day, and while I knew that he was as motivated as anyone to figure out who was behind the bomb, I didn't want him to overdo.

"I suppose I could use a break." Kyle glanced out the window. "The rain and snow showers have stopped, and the sun is out. Maybe we can bundle up and sit on the back deck while the dogs get some exercise."

"That sounds like a perfect plan. I'll grab some blankets."

The estate Kyle owned was located in an isolated cove on Paradise Lake. Jeremiah Collins, the man who brought residents to the area when he opened a lumber mill more than a hundred years ago, had built the huge home. Kyle had inherited the estate from his grandfather, Zachary Collins, four years ago. He'd completely remodeled it since then, but the exquisite location amongst the only grove of old growth trees left in the area was really something to behold.

"This is nice," I said after tucking a blanket around Kyle and then snuggling in beside him. "Things have been so hectic since the explosion. And so stressful. I feel like I really haven't had a chance to catch my breath."

"Things have been intense. I feel like I am missing an entire chunk of time."

"The explosion was just three days ago. Not all that long in the grand scheme of things, but with everything we've had to deal with, it seems a lot longer."

Kyle wove his fingers through mine. "I guess I missed Gracie's presentation at school on Wednesday."

My youngest sister, Gracie, had been assigned a presentation relating to the history of the Paradise Lake area, and she'd chosen to do her speech about Kyle's family and the impact they'd had on the entire area when they brought commerce and jobs to the area.

"I talked Hunter into releasing me from my overnight stay in time to make it to the presentation," I informed Kyle. "She did really well. The information and photos you provided to her made her speech by far the best of any of those presented."

"I'm really sorry I missed it."

I tucked the blanket up under my chin to ward off the slight breeze. "Me too but there will be other presentations to attend. In fact, I think Ashley has a founder's day event after the first of the year, and, of course, Gracie has the Thanksgiving play in a couple of weeks."

Kyle adjusted his position slightly. He was trying to put on a brave face, but I could see that he was still in a fair amount of pain. Deciding that leaning against him probably wasn't the best position for us to be in, I got up and sat down on a chair across from him. The fact that he didn't argue for me to remain by his side confirmed my suspicion.

"Speaking of Ashley, how did her date go?" Kyle asked after I was settled in the chair. "The poor thing was about as nervous as I've ever seen her when she left on Tuesday."

"I think it went well. If you remember, there were eight of them, four couples. Jenna dropped Ashley and Kristi off at the burger place next to the movie theater. Ashley said the food was good, but the movie was boring, although it didn't seem she really cared that the movie was boring. She said she had a good time."

Kyle smiled. "She is growing up so fast. I still remember the little girl I met on that first Halloween. She was so concerned about how to fit in and what sort of costume was best for someone who was most definitely no longer a baby."

"Not being seen as a baby has always been a big theme for her," I smiled at the memory.

"She's had a tough go of it, but she found a way to fit into her new life after your mom died. It seems like only yesterday she was trying to find her way on that first Halloween and now she is dating. It's crazy."

"She's not dating in the conventional sense," I countered. "Jenna dropped her off and picked her up. She attended the dinner and the movie with Kristi and six other friends. I mean, technically, the friends did pair up, and the outing was referred to as a date, but it wasn't actually a date. Was it?"

Kyle grinned. "I think it was."

I groaned. "I guess you're right. Our baby is growing up so fast. Before you know it, she'll be going off to college and then we'll never see her."

"We'll see her. She told me that she wants to go to Stanford. That isn't all that far away."

I made a face. "Even if she gets in, which is far from being a given, Stanford is pretty pricy. I'm not sure I'll be able to swing that even with the money I've squirreled away to pay for the girls' college."

Kyle paused. He made a face I couldn't quite read but seemed to convey hesitation. "I know we agreed to take things slowly, and I'm very willing to do that, but I sort of hoped that by the time Ashley was ready for college, our relationship would have matured to the point where we would naturally pay for her college together."

I frowned.

"Ashley won't go to college for almost six years," Kyle pointed out. "Surely, you see us being married by then?"

I leaned back into my chair as I tried to gather my thoughts.

"Tj?" Kyle asked.

I glanced at the man sitting across from me. The longer I took to respond, the more serious his expression grew. I could sense the tension between us exponentially increase as he waited for my answer, yet I still couldn't find the words to end his torment.

"Tj?" Kyle asked once again.

I took a deep breath and forced a smile. "Yes, of course, I see us as being married by then. I'm not sure why the whole thing caught me off guard. I guess I just never stopped to really think about a timeline." I furrowed my brow as I tried to wrap my head around things. "Have you? Thought of a timeline that is?"

Kyle hesitated. He appeared to be taking a moment to think about his response before answering. Eventually, he spoke in a slow and level tone of voice. "No. Not really. Or I guess I should say, not specifically, but when I look into the future, I see us — you and me and Ashley and Gracie — living together as a family. And I will admit that when I spoke to Ashley about Stanford, it never entered my mind that we wouldn't be married by the time she went off to college. Am I to assume by your complete surprise when I suggested as much, that I've imagined things differently than you've envisioned?"

I had no idea what to say. The conversation had taken a turn I really wasn't expecting, and while I really did want to respond to Kyle, my mind simply wouldn't form the words needed to prevent this conversation from becoming even more awkward than it already was.

"It's okay if you haven't thought that far ahead," Kyle assured me. "I really didn't mean to bring up such a delicate subject at this particular point in time."

"No, it's okay." I paused and then continued. "While it is true that I have not looked quite as far into the future as you have, I do love you, and I do think about us being a family one day." I took a deep breath and blew it out slowly. "I'm not sure why the whole thing hit me wrong. Of course, I want to marry you, but not now. Dad and Rosalie are getting married next month, and we don't want to overshadow their wedding, but maybe next summer, or even in the fall."

Kyle raised a brow. "Next fall? Are you ready to talk about a date?"

I glanced at the man who had he always been there for me. I felt nothing but love for the man who'd followed me across the country and back when I'd been so torn up about another guy that I'd decided to leave Paradise Lake. I felt my heart skip a beat as I thought about Kyle's patience and kindness. I smiled and nodded. "I suppose discussing a date might seem abrupt. I realize there is a protocol which most feel should be upheld, and I know that technically I am bypassing the whole you getting down on one knee followed by a syrupy speech thing, but I don't need that. To be honest, I don't even want that. We've both had complicated relationships in the past, but to this point, our relationship has been mostly easy and uncomplicated. You are my best friend. I love you. I think that on some level I have always loved you. I want to spend my life with you. We could wait and do things in a more traditional manner, but my heart is telling me that if we both want to get married, we should cut to the chase and get married."

"Just like that?"

I nodded. "Just like that."

# CHAPTER 6

Saturday, November 11

It had been a week since Harriet's funeral. Lloyd had been buried the day after Harriet, and Bookman had awakened the day after that. Hank was still in a coma and not expected to awaken at this point. As for our spontaneous engagement, Kyle and I had decided to wait to make an announcement until everyone was together on Thanksgiving. I could tell that Kyle was thrown by our sudden decision to move from dating to planning a wedding, but he wanted me to be happy, and I assured him that a no muss, no fuss sort of transition was what I wanted. He offered to buy me any ring I wanted, but I decided that the ring I wanted to wear was the ring Zachary had given to Kyle's grandmother, Mary, even though they had never been legally married. Still, the ring was gorgeous, and given its history, it made me feel close not only to Kyle but also to his heritage. Of course, since we hadn't told anyone that we were engaged, I couldn't wear the ring yet, but waiting to tell everyone at our Thanksgiving feast seemed like a good idea, so I was happy to delay the unveiling until our special day.

"Can I come in?" Gracie poked her head in through a crack in the opening of my previously closed bedroom door.

"Sure honey. Come on in." I pulled a corner of my heavy

comforter back so that Gracie could snuggle under the covers with me. "You're up early."

"Pumpkin needed to go out, so I had to get up. I think her stomach is feeling rumbly."

Pumpkin was Gracie's golden retriever.

"Have you been feeding her people food again?"

"Not a lot. I guess I gave her some cheese last night. And I let her lick my ice cream bowl when I was done eating."

"Pumpkin has a delicate stomach, so you need to be careful about what you give her. She doesn't seem to do well with dairy products, so cheese and ice cream probably weren't a good idea."

Gracie laid her head on my shoulder. I wrapped my arm around both her and the stuffed bunny she'd clung to. She'd always been my snuggle bunny, and I dreaded the day she would decide she was too old for these heart-to-heart talks, but so far, she seemed to enjoy them as much as I did.

"Will you make her chicken and rice?" Gracie asked after a minute. "The last time she was sick, you made her a big pot of it, and by the time the pot was gone, she was feeling better."

"I'll make some before we go into town. Are you still going over to Kari's?"

"Actually, Kari is coming here. Kristi too. Jenna is going over to her mom's house to sit with Bookman while Helen goes to the hairdresser."

I frowned. "I thought Helen hired a nurse to help out when Bookman came home."

"Ashley said that Bookman said no to a nurse. She told me that at first Kari's grandma wasn't happy about having to take care of Bookman all by herself, but Kari told me yesterday that Helen was so happy to have Bookman home, that she decided she didn't really care about having help."

"I guess if Kristi and Kari are coming over here today, I'll need to change my plans. I'm kind of surprised that Jenna didn't call and let me know about the change ahead of time."

"You don't have to change your plans. Rosalie is watching us. In fact, it was Rosalie's idea to have Kristi and Kari over so that Jenna could help her mom out."

Okay. On the one hand, I wasn't sure how I felt about Rosalie changing plans I had set up without even checking with me. On the other hand, Helen probably did need a break, and it made sense that Jenna should focus on being there for her family. The reality was that I should have realized as much in the first place. "I guess we should get up and see how Pumpkin is doing. I'll check with Rosalie and see if she needs help today. Once I do that, I'll make chicken and rice for both Echo and Pumpkin. You know Echo isn't going to want dog food once he smells the chicken cooking."

"The cat's like chicken as well," Gracie pointed out.

I was beginning to suspect that Pumpkin didn't even have a stomachache. I wouldn't be at all surprised to find out that Gracie made the whole thing up just to score a home cooked meal for the Jensen family animals on this cold and snowy Saturday morning. The reality was that making up a story to score a treat for the animals was precisely the sort of thing I would have done when I was her age, so I really couldn't be mad about it.

By the time Gracie and I arrived in the kitchen, Grandpa had chicken boiling in a pot and pancakes on the griddle. I guess he must have heard about Pumpkin's rumbly tummy as well. I poured myself a cup of coffee and sat down across from Ashley and Rosalie, who were talking about a sewing project.

"I understand there has been a change of plans and Kristi and Kari are coming over here today," I said to Rosalie, who had the day off from the veterinary clinic she ran with her new partner.

Rosalie nodded. "I hope that is okay. I'll be here, so you don't need to change your plans."

"It's fine." I took a sip of my coffee. "It was very nice of you to want to help Helen. Do you need help today?"

Rosalie shook her head. "I think we have it under control. Ashley and Kristi want to learn to make a jean purse like the one we saw in town. I thought I'd help them. Your dad is going to take Gracie and Kari to buy their costumes for the Thanksgiving play the school is producing and then to a movie since the resort is closed and he has the day off."

"I wasn't aware the school was asking the students to buy their costumes for the play."

Rosalie nodded. "With the budget cuts, it seemed to be the best option. The staff purchased the costumes, and they will be on hand today for the students who have been cast to stop by with an adult to pay for the items ordered for them. Gracie is going to be a pilgrim girl."

"Yes, she told me. And I am happy to take both her and Kari to buy their costumes. Dad doesn't have to give up his day off."

Rosalie put her hand over mine. "I think he wants to spend the day with the girls. These girls are growing up so fast that I know we both feel the need to get in as much grandparent time as we can before they are off to college, and we never see them anymore."

Okay, that felt like a dagger to my heart. Hadn't I just said the same thing to Kyle?

"By the way," Rosalie changed the subject. "I ran into Frannie in town yesterday, and she mentioned Thanksgiving. I know that she is usually invited to the resort, so I assumed she was welcome at Kyle's as well. I told her about the change this year, but you might want to follow up."

"I will. Thanks. And yes, everyone who usually comes here will be welcome there."

"I hoped you'd let me do the turkeys this year. I know you don't like to cook, and Jenna seems to have her hands full."

Okay, I experienced a flash of irritation that it seemed like Rosalie was trying to take the whole thing over, but she was right, I didn't like to cook, nor was I particularly good at it, and Jenna did have her hands full. "Thank you. That would be very helpful. Kyle has double ovens, but we'll need to use those for the sides. I guess a meal this size will be a bit more challenging since we won't have the commercial ovens in The Grill that we normally use."

Rosalie smiled. "I think we can manage if everyone pitches in. I am happy to help with pies and rolls as well. Really, if you need anything at all, you just need to ask."

I forced a smile. "Jenna usually brings the dessert, so I'm sure she is planning on bringing the pies, but help with the rolls would be welcomed. Thank you."

"I'm just happy to be part of things."

I smiled and nodded. Shortly after, Rosalie excused herself to head upstairs and get dressed. Ashley followed, leaving just Gracie and me with Grandpa.

"Did you already mention the change in our Thanksgiving venue to Doc?" Grandpa asked as he slid two fluffy golden pancakes onto my plate.

"I did. Jenna let Bookman and her mom know about our plans. I think she planned to call Bree and Pastor Dan. If she hasn't, I will. Please do let me know if anyone specific comes to mind. I don't want to miss anyone."

"Are you sure you want to do this?" Grandpa asked as he handed me the warm syrup. "You already seem to have a lot on your plate with the investigation into the bombing."

I nodded as I poured syrup over the pancakes. I picked up a piece of bacon and took a bite. "I'm sure I want to do this. It will be a lot of work, and at first, I was less than certain that we should take it on, but it was Kyle's idea, and it seems to be important to him." I sliced off a piece of the pancake and took my first bite of the drippy sweet cake. "These are delicious."

"Same as I make every week."

I took another bite. "And they are always delicious."

"Grandpa makes the best pancakes in the whole world," Gracie agreed.

Grandpa smiled. "Thank you, darlin'."

"Do you have plans with Doc today?" I asked after Grandpa refilled my coffee without my even having to ask.

"The two of us are going to talk to some folks we figure could have been in the area when the town hall blew up. We know that finding anyone who actually saw anything is a longshot, especially since Roy and Kate have already canvassed the area, but we don't feel right about sitting around and doing nothing."

"I get that."

"Folks keep telling us that we should let the professionals handle things. They say there is nothing we can do, but all this waiting around is for the birds."

"Kyle and I feel the same way. In fact, I am heading over to Kyle's to work on it as soon as I can get ready. If you and Doc want to come by, or if you come up with anything and want to run it past us, just give me a ring. We'll do the same if we come up with something."

Grandpa's expression turned serious. "You have yourself a deal. One way or another, the person behind this is going to pay."

After I was done eating, I finished cooking and assembling the chicken and rice Grandpa had started. Then I fed the two dogs and four cats before heading upstairs to shower and dress. While I did intend to head over to Kyle's as I'd told Grandpa, I wanted to check in with Jenna first to see how she was doing. I guess I had been pretty wrapped up in my own stuff as of late, but it really should have been me who thought to check in with Helen and Jenna and not the step-witch who had taken over my house.

# CHAPTER 7

"I'm the worst person ever," I said to Jenna two hours later after we settled in at her kitchen table with cups of coffee.

"The worst person ever? Wow, that's quite a claim. I imagine you have some sort of evidence to back up such a grandiose statement?"

I wrapped my hands around the coffee mug Jenna had set in front of me. "Not only have I totally neglected you this past week, even though you have been dealing with something huge, but I spent half the morning entertaining mean thoughts about Rosalie because she actually had the wherewithal to check in with you, which was a wonderful and thoughtful thing to do, but somehow her kind gesture made me angry."

"Angry?"

"You are my best friend, and Ashley and Gracie are my sisters, and Rosalie is being a better friend to you, and sister to them, than I am."

Jenna chuckled. "You really are a mess. Are you sure that beam that fell on you didn't hit you on the head before it pinned your leg?"

I rolled my eyes. "I know. I'm still doing it. I don't really understand why I am annoyed by everything this perfectly lovely person does."

"If you ask me, I think there are too many queen bees in the hive."

I lifted a brow. "Queen bees?"

"Even though you were the daughter and not the wife, you have been the woman of the house since your mom left when you were three. Your position has never once been challenged until Rosalie came along and assumed her role as your father's future wife. She has now moved into the position of queen bee since he owns the house, which has left you feeling displaced."

"You think?"

Jenna nodded. "I do. And it is natural that you might feel that way. I can see that you are trying to make it work, as is Rosalie, and for your father's sake, I hope that you will continue to try even when you feel that your toes have been stomped on."

I let out a breath. "I guess I can try to remember that Rosalie actually is the queen bee in my father's house. I will admit that I have been having a hard time with the whole thing, but thankfully, I won't have to deal with the situation for much longer."

"Come again?" Jenna asked. "What do you mean you won't have to deal with the situation for much longer? You aren't planning to get rid of this perfectly lovely woman, are you?"

Now I had to chuckle. "No, I'm not getting rid of Rosalie. What I meant is that I won't be living at the resort for much longer."

"So you have decided to move in with Kyle?"

I nodded. "Actually, we are engaged."

Jenna's eyes doubled in size. "Engaged. Really?"

I nodded again.

She screamed and hugged me. "My god Tj, why didn't you tell me?"

"It happened sort of fast, and we decided not to tell anyone until Thanksgiving. Still, I should have called you right away."

Jenna hugged me again. "Yes, you should have. When did it happen?"

"A week ago yesterday. We were catching up, and somehow we got onto the subject of college and the cost of sending the girls to a good one, and the next thing I know we were talking about getting hitched."

Jenna frowned. "Maybe you should walk me through this."

"There is nothing to walk through. It was all pretty unspectacular. Kyle mentioned that Ashley wanted to go to Stanford, and I made a comment about how expensive that would be. He responded by pointing out that Stanford or any college Ashley might decide to go to was an expense that was quite a few years away. I guess I didn't understand the significance of this statement and must have looked confused because then he pointed out that we'd be married by then and as a married couple, we would pay for Ashley's college tuition together. When I didn't answer right away, I could see that look of panic he gets when he realizes that maybe we aren't at the same point in the relationship. I hate that look. I love Kyle, and I fully intend to marry him. I really don't know why I have been making him take every aspect of our relationship so slow. I'm not exactly sure how it happened, but I found myself telling Kyle that yes, I would marry him even though he never actually asked."

"And that's it? He didn't get down on one knee or present you with a fancy ring?"

I shook my head.

"And you are okay with that?"

I thought about Kyle's sweet smile and the fact that I really wanted our transition from dating to engaged to be as easy as it could be. "Yes. I am more than okay with that."

Jenna's face softened as her long blond hair fell across one eye. She used a finger to tuck it behind her ear. "I can't believe you are engaged." She hugged me again, squeezing me even harder than she had before.

"I realize this is sort of off the cuff, but so far this whole wedding thing has been off the cuff. I have no idea when we will actually be married, but when we do get around to it, I would be honored if you would be my matron of honor."

A tear ran down Jenna's cheek. "Of course, I'll be your matron of honor. You are like a sister to me, and Kyle is one of the best people I know. I love the fact that you finally found each other. I know he will make you as happy as you deserve to be."

I realized I was happy. As happy as I'd ever been. Or at least I would be, once I'd tracked down the maniac who had killed two people.

"We have so much planning to do." Jenna rubbed her hands together in a manner that communicated quite clearly that she was ready and able to get started.

Suddenly everything was becoming very real. "I'm super excited to be marrying Kyle, and I want to share everything about this with you, but honestly with everything that is going on, bridesmaid dresses and flower arrangements are the last things on my mind. Besides, at this point, no one other than you knows that Kyle and I are engaged, so let's put a pin in the whole planning thing."

"I get that. And you have plenty of time. I promise I won't crowd you. Has any progress been made in regard to the investigation into the explosion?"

"Not a lot," I admitted. "Kyle has Lloyd's computer. It took him a few days to get past the password, but he finally got in. While there were five council members present on the night of the explosion, Lloyd was the most controversial of the five, so we figured that the blast might have been related to something he was working on."

"And did you find anything?"

I shrugged. "Not really. Kyle is still going through all the files. Apparently, there are a lot of files to sort through, and some of the files have additional security. He did find plans for a condominium development along Snowshoe Beach that he seems to be working on with James Kingston. I'm sure that if such a project was ever made public, it would cause a lot of controversy. I mean really, aren't there enough condos in the area, and even if it was determined that additional housing was warranted, why on earth would you destroy such a lovely lakefront property?"

Jenna frowned. "Had Kyle heard about the project prior to accessing Lloyd's computer?"

"No. He said it appeared that the plans for the project were in the early stages."

"I thought the Boatman family owned all that land. Surely, they wouldn't sell."

Jenna had a point. The land in the area of Snowshoe Beach had been owned by the Boatman family for generations. It was odd that Lloyd and Kingston had plans to build there. I suppose it was possible the land might have been sold, but something about the whole thing felt wrong. "Now that you mention it, a new development on that property does seem odd. Although I suppose it is unlikely that the condo project was behind the blast since it seems unlikely Lloyd shared his plans with anyone beyond his inner circle."

"I agree. It's probably not related." Jenna got up and refilled my coffee. I was going to be floating by the end of the morning, but there were days when massive amounts of coffee seemed called for, and this was one of those days. "I heard that Lloyd had been pushing the council hard to approach a man he had worked with in the past about the position of mayor. Maybe the whole controversy relating to the position is behind the blast."

I considered this. "Kyle didn't mention anything about a prospective candidate for mayor, so my sense is that Lloyd was just trying to make a power play that never went anywhere." I blew out a breath of frustration. "It is so hard to know what might have caused someone to do what they did. I know Bookman has only been out of his coma for five days, but I wonder if he has said whether or not he remembers anything about the events of the night of the explosion."

"I haven't spoken to him about the explosion, but I do know that Roy went to the hospital and spoke to him shortly after he regained consciousness." Jenna poured coffee grounds into the coffee maker and started another pot. "Based on what Dennis told me after he spoke to Roy, Bookman didn't remember a thing after he arrived at the town hall before the meeting began. I suppose that is natural. He did receive a severe blow to the head. It is actually amazing his memory wasn't affected more than it was."

"Have you heard if he knew why Harriet called the meeting in the first place?"

Jenna knit her brow. "I'm not sure. You should talk to Roy. He knows more about it than I do."

"It seems odd to me that an emergency meeting was even called on Halloween night. People had plans. It seems to me that unless there was some sort of a life and death situation to deal with, Harriet and whichever council member asked for the meeting, would have waited until the next day."

"The timing does seem odd. Maybe if you can figure out who called the meeting, you can figure out who placed the bomb in the town hall."

"I hope so. I think that at this point, everyone is getting pretty frustrated with our lack of progress."

Jenna glanced at the clock. "I really do want to help out with the bombing investigation, and I'm ecstatic about your news, but I need to head over to mom's place. If she is late for her hair appointment, she isn't going to be easy to live with. But

I do want to talk to you some more about everything. Maybe we can get a drink later."

"I'd like that. Text me when you get home from your mom's."

# CHAPTER 8

After leaving Jenna's, I decided to stop at the store. Kyle's food supplies were at an all-time low, and it didn't make sense for us to go out for every meal. I was heading toward the produce aisle when I ran into a woman who used to work at The Antiquery with Jenna.

"Denise. How are you?" I asked the petite blond with bright green eyes.

"I'm good. Busy. The diner is slammed this week with so many tourists being in town for the holiday and with the kids out of school, it has been total chaos. I heard about the explosion. Are you and Kyle okay?"

"I came out of it with a few bumps and bruises, and while Kyle had to spend a couple of days in the hospital, he is doing fine now as well."

Denise's smile faded. "I was so sorry to hear about Harriet and Lloyd."

"Losing those we cared about has been difficult," I agreed.

"And as bad as the loss of human life is, the aftershock of the total destruction of the town offices has everyone on edge. I tried to renew my business license and pay my local tax when it was due, but the town is basically closed for business, so at this point, I'm just hanging onto the check. I know other business owners are feeling as lost as I am."

"Kyle is trying to get things back on track, but it will take a while. In the meantime, he will need everyone's patience."

Denise tossed the can of tuna she'd had in her hand when I'd walked up into her cart. "I guess a first step would be to appoint new council members. There is a rumor going around that James Kingston is circulating a petition which would require the town council to be elected by popular vote rather than appointed. To be honest, I'm not even sure he can do that, but apparently, he is trying."

I paused to think about Kingston's plan. "Currently and in the past, the sitting council has voted amongst themselves to fill any open seats. I know Kyle is working on doing that. I don't know for certain what the bylaws say, but I assume there is some sort of a provision which allows residents to add measures to the local ballot. I'll have to ask Kyle about it,"

"My first thought was that Kingston wasn't even a resident, so he shouldn't be able to add items to our ballot. But then a friend pointed out that he does own property within the town limits. A lot of it. My friend seemed to think that owning property entitles him to vote, but I'm really not sure if she is right or wrong about that."

"I think that voting is based on residency and you can only be a resident of one state, county, and town, but I might be wrong. I've never looked into it."

"Kingston seems like a smart guy, so I imagine he must have looked into the legalities of circulating a petition to have a measure added to the ballot," Denise pointed out. "Of course, the next election isn't until June, but I suppose he saw an opening and decided to jump on it."

"I guess he might have."

"I support the idea that anyone who has enough support can ask that an issue is put out to the voters, but you know Kingston is doing what he is because he thinks he can fill the council with men who will vote the way he wants them to vote.

Having said that, I do think an elected council is a good idea. In the past, the council has always been a governing board made up of longtime residents who want things done a certain way, but, if you ask me, it's time for a change. If the measure does make it to the June ballot, I will vote for elected seats on the council with term limits, but I can guarantee you that I won't be voting for anyone who supports turning our little town into a tourist mecca."

I could see that the idea of electing town council members was going to be an emotional one on both sides, and while I didn't disagree with Denise, I really didn't want to get into a political debate right here in the middle of a crowded grocery store. I was about to suggest a topic change when Denise announced that she had to run. After Denise scurried off, I finished picking up the items I needed and then got into the long line at the checkout counter. I wondered if Kyle knew about the petition Kingston was circulating. I wondered what he thought about the idea if he did know. Kyle was a pretty open-minded guy. I actually thought he might support the idea of an elected town council.

After I finished my errands, I headed toward Kyle's home, where I found him chatting with Jeff. I was thrilled to see that Jeff was doing better. During those first few days when everyone was in the hospital, I wondered if any of the council members other than Kyle would be able to return to active duty with the town.

"You look a lot better than the last time I saw you," I teased.

Jeff put a hand to his face, which still bore evidence of the cuts and abrasions he'd suffered. "Hunter has assured me that while I may have a few scars to serve as a reminder of the horrific night, I should make a full recovery."

I gave Jeff a careful hug. "I'm happy to hear that."

"Jeff and I are trying to figure out what needs to be done to keep the town open," Kyle said.

"Which is going to be harder than it might seem," Jeff added. "Harriet, who has been the mayor's secretary and town clerk for decades, is gone, the mayor in charge is barely out of the hospital and in no shape to be bothered with town business, and the other two senior town council members are either dead or unconscious. I've only been on the council for two months and Kyle for two years, but at this point, we are all the town has."

I sat down across from the men who were sitting at the dining table. "Can I help?"

"Maybe," Kyle answered. "At this point, not only do we need to figure out what needs to be done, but we also need to come up with a plan to do it. If you stop and think about it, the town is completely crippled. There are independent contractors to pay, proposals before the town council to be voted on, and day-to-day decisions to make. It will be months and months before the council is able to follow through with any of the projects we were in the middle of implementing or vote on any of the issues we'd been discussing."

"Which, if you stop to think about it, has benefited James Kingston quite nicely," I added.

"It does seem that the timing of everything that is going on has worked out for the guy," Jeff agreed.

"I ran into a friend at the market who told me that James Kingston is circulating a petition to change the town's bylaws so that the seats on the town council will be elected positions with term limits. Had you heard about that?" I asked Kyle.

"After the dust settled following the explosion, Kingston came to me with a list of names of men he wanted to see added to the council to fill the three open seats," Kyle informed us. "The men on the list were all on his payroll, and it seemed apparent to me that none of the men he supported would care about town business beyond the vacation rental issue. The town really needs council members who will care about the town as a whole, so I thanked him and told him that I was going in another direction. He told me that he had read the town's bylaws which allowed for any resident to add a measure to the local ballot if they were able to gather enough signatures. He threatened to support a change to the bylaws which would require an elected council with term limits if I didn't play his game."

"Kingston isn't a resident," I pointed out.

"Maybe not, but he has employees who are. He'd just need to put their name on the ballot."

"So is this a real threat?" Jeff asked.

"Not as far as I'm concerned," Kyle answered. "In my opinion, if the majority of the town's residents want to see elected positions, then maybe it is time for a change."

"Maybe but you know that Kingston is just trying to stack the council with people who will support his business ventures," Jeff pointed out.

Kyle nodded. "I know that stacking the council is his goal, but keep in mind that the citizens who live here still have to vote for the change in the bylaws, and even if that change passes the popular vote, the registered voters still need to elect the candidates they feel would do the best job. I think we should trust the people who live in the area to know what is best for them."

Kyle was right. It did seem that the residents of Serenity would be able to figure out that Kingston was up to no good. I picked up an envelope that had been sitting near Kyle's elbow. "What's this?"

"It is a certified letter that was dropped off this morning."

"Certified letter from whom?" I asked.

"Kingston's attorney," Kyle answered. "He is threatening to

sue the town and the individual members of the town council if a ban on vacation rentals is put into place. The letter is dated October 31st."

I narrowed my gaze. "Lloyd had lunch with Kingston on the day of the explosion, so Kingston must have given him a heads up about his plans to sue everyone which might very well be why Lloyd decided to call the emergency meeting."

"It seems like it could have waited," I said.

"Maybe," Kyle agreed. "Not only was Lloyd Kingston's friend and colleague, but he was also a town council member. After meeting with Kingston, Lloyd might have decided to let the council members know what was going on before the letter could be delivered."

I paused to let this sink in. "That does make sense. As a developer, Lloyd was very much against the ban. He may have gotten together with Kingston to make a power play. If I had to guess, Lloyd asked Harriet to call the meeting at which time he planned to present a grim picture of a lengthy court case that would cost the town as well as the individual town council members thousands of dollars."

Kyle nodded. "Lloyd was a very articulate and impassioned man. I'm sure he would have made a heck of a case that the council should just drop the idea of banning vacation rentals before it ended up costing everyone a lot of money."

"So why is this letter just being delivered to you now?" I asked.

"Once the town hall was destroyed, there was nowhere to deliver mail, so it has been held either at the post office, as in this case, or by the courier service. I spoke to Hazel yesterday, and we opened a post office box for the US mail sent to the town. I have let everyone I can think of, know if they have deliveries or packages to take them to the post office as well. I'm sure it will take a while for word to get out about the temporary address. I anticipate that mail and deliveries will continue to trickle in for months."

"I can't say for sure that Kingston would blow up the town hall, but everything does seem to be circling back around to him," Jeff pointed out. "At the very least, I think we should try to get a look at his banking and phone records."

I looked at Kyle. "Did you ever find out who had been calling Lloyd in the days leading up to the explosion? With everything else we have been juggling, I forgot about the calls until Jeff just brought up the subject."

"The calls were from a burner that had been purchased by Lloyd."

"Lloyd. Why would Lloyd be receiving calls from a phone he purchased?"

"I guess he bought it and gave it to someone for the purpose of communicating with him," Kyle answered.

That did make sense. I should have thought of that. "So the calls are a dead end?"

Kyle nodded. "Unless new information is made available to us, then I would say yes, the calls are a dead end."

"We do have a lot of evidence to suggest that Lloyd and Kingston were in cahoots to a certain degree," Jeff pointed out. "Maybe that information can be used to strong-arm Kingston into telling what he knows."

Kyle bobbed his head slightly. "I suppose that Roy might want to take a closer look at Kingston, and it does seem possible that he knows more than he has said at this point, but the reason we are meeting today is to come up with a plan to get the town back in business."

"You're right," Jeff agreed. "It is easy to get distracted. Where do we start?"

"It seems to me that the first step is to appoint new members to the council," Kyle answered. "We need to find replacements for Lloyd, who is definitely not going to be back, and Hank, who is most likely not going to be back, and we still have that open seat to deal with."

"Okay," Jeff agreed. "Any suggestions?"

"What about Brandon Halliwell," Kyle said. Brandon owned one-half of Guns and Roses, a combination flower shop and guns and ammo store, along with his sister, Rita.

"Brandon is a good choice," Jeff agreed. "He has lived in the area for a long time, he seems to know most of the locals, and he has a good head on his shoulders."

"What about Rita?" I asked. "She is all of those things as well."

"I don't think that it would be a good idea to have a brother and sister team on the council, but both would make good candidates," Kyle answered. "I think we should add both Brandon and Rita to our list. What about Nick Grainger? He has lived in the area longer than almost anyone." Nick owned Grainger General Store along with his wife, Emma.

"Nick has the background that would make him a good candidate, but he is getting on in years, and I know he is looking to sell the store so he and Emma can retire," I informed the men. "What about David Harris?" David owned the local pharmacy.

"David would be a good option," Kyle said. "We'll add him to the list as well."

The room fell into silence as we all considered the question at hand. I could hear the tick-tock of the old grandfather clock that had sat at the foot of the stairs since before I'd first met Zachary. There were actually three council positions to fill in addition to finding a mayor, and finding the best people to fill those positions was going to be key.

"What about Greg Remington," Jeff suggested, after a moment. "He hasn't lived in the area as long as some of the others, but he is a hard worker who is well-liked and respected in the community." Greg was the principal of the high school where I worked. We all agreed that he'd be a good candidate.

The three of us continued to discuss options. It was decided that if Bookman was up for it, Kyle and Jeff would make a list and then discuss the options with him before they tried to put the men and women on the list in any sort of order. As for the town clerk/mayor's secretary position, Kyle suggested that they post an advertisement for the position and see who applied. Once the list of candidates seemed complete, I decided to ask Jeff about his memories of the night of the explosion. I knew that Kyle wanted to focus on town business, but in my mind, finding the person who killed Harriet and Lloyd was the most important subject of all.

"Harriet texted me about the meeting. I was just closing up my shop, so I headed directly over. When I arrived, Lloyd was already in the council chambers. I asked him what was up and he said he didn't know, although I had the distinct impression that he did know and just wasn't ready to talk about it. Bookman came in shortly after, and Harriet came in a few minutes later. Hank came in next, and then you and Kyle came in last, but no one ever did say why we were there. My impression was that whatever was going on was a big deal, and Harriet wanted to wait to fill us in until everyone was there."

"Did you notice a package or backpack in the room?" I asked.

Jeff shook his head. "No. I wasn't looking for one, but nothing stood out as being odd. Harriet had that big purse she always carries. She put it in the drawer of her desk, but I didn't notice that anyone else brought anything in with them."

"Was anyone in attendance acting oddly?" I wondered. "Unusually nervous or perhaps impatient?"

"No," Jeff answered. "Lloyd had a serious look on his face,

and his tone of voice was sort of flat, but Lloyd can be taciturn at the best of times. Bookman was his usual happy self, but Harriet seemed sort of distracted. I had the feeling she wanted to hurry things along. When Hank first walked in, he seemed irritated about being pulled away from the restaurant, but then he started joking around with Bookman and lightened up considerably."

"And during the time you were there, did anyone else other than council members enter the building?" I asked.

"Other than you, no."

# CHAPTER 9

After Jeff left, Kyle and I entered into a discussion about how we wanted to spend our day, but shortly after Jeff drove away, Roy pulled up in his police cruiser, so we put our plans on hold in order to speak to him.

"Do you have news?" I asked after inviting Roy in and offering him coffee.

"I do," Roy confirmed. "Most of it is good, but some is not so good."

I sat down on the sofa across from where Roy sat next to Kyle. "So what's up?"

Roy took a sip of his coffee and then set the mug on the table in front of him before he answered. "First of all, Hank woke up."

I smiled. "That's great. When I spoke to Hunter the other day, he told me he wasn't sure he would."

Roy rested his elbows on his knees and based on the expression on his face, I had to assume that the not so good news was actually bad news. I figured it was best to give Roy the time he needed to work up to saying what he needed to, so I just sat quietly.

"According to Hunter," Roy began, "while Hank is conscious and responsive to verbal cues, he has a long recovery ahead of him. Not only is he paralyzed from the waist down, but at this point, he is unable to speak, although it is Hunter's opinion that he will regain the ability to speak over time. As for walking, he isn't certain. They are moving him to a larger hospital off the mountain where they can deal with his long-term care better. Hunter shared with me the fact that he won't be at all surprised to find that Hank will never again be able to resume normal activities such as running the restaurant or sitting on the town council."

Poor Hank. "I guess we should be happy that he pulled through, but if he doesn't regain the use of his legs, it is going to be tough on him."

Roy sighed. "Yeah. It is difficult to think of the big Texan in a wheelchair. Still, I imagine that life in a wheelchair is better than no life at all."

"Were you able to ask him about the night of the explosion?" I realized the odds of him knowing anything were slim, but I still felt the need to ask.

"I tried. I hoped he could nod in response to my questions, but he just looked confused when I brought it up. I don't think he remembers anything. At least not at this point."

"Maybe with time." I glanced at Kyle, who had a look of contemplation on his face. "Anything else?"

Roy bobbed his head slowly. "I was able to speak to the crime scene guys who did have a few of the pieces we were missing. The most interesting thing I discovered is that it looks like the bomb was brought into the building in the purse Harriet was carrying. We don't know for certain that the bomb was in her purse, but we do know that the explosion originated from the location where her purse was stored."

"Jeff mentioned that she had brought her purse into the meeting," I informed Roy. "He said she put it in her desk drawer. Wouldn't she have noticed the additional weight if it had been added to her purse?"

Roy answered. "The bomb wasn't all that large and most

likely didn't weigh all that much, but the raw materials that were used made it a powerful one. At this point, we are assuming that the device was made by someone with a background in munitions. What we don't know is if the person who made the bomb was the one to plant it in Harriet's purse, or if the person who did the planting simply purchased the bomb from a dealer of some sort."

"Was the bomb set up with a timer or a detonator?" I asked.

"It looks like a timer was used, which means that we really have no way of knowing if the person who slipped the bomb into Harriet's purse even intended to blow up the town hall with the members of the town council inside. The meeting had been a last-minute development, and there is really no way to know when the bomb was slipped into Harriet's purse, if that is in fact, what happened. On the one hand, I suppose it is possible that the bomb was slipped into her purse after the meeting was called, and the bomber knew exactly where Harriet's purse would be and who would be in proximity to her at the time of the explosion. On the other hand, if it had been disguised, the bomb could have been added to her purse earlier in the day. I don't think we can eliminate the possibility that it was the bomber's intention that the bomb detonate after Harriet returned home for the evening."

I wasn't liking the sound of that at all. Could Harriet have been the intended victim? If so, I couldn't think of a single person who would want her dead. If you asked me, Harriet as the intended victim made a lot less sense than either Lloyd, or the council as a whole, as the intended victim, but still...

"Not knowing which scenario is true is going to complicate the investigation," I pointed out. "It seems to me that the list of suspects who might want to kill an entire town council is going to be very different from the list of suspects who might want to kill an individual woman who might work for the town, but is also a neighbor, friend, and relative."

Roy leaned forward, resting his forearms on his thighs. "The ambiguity of the target does make this increasingly difficult. It may be a longshot, but it seems like it might be beneficial to speak to Helen if I can get her to open up."

"Helen?" I asked.

"She was Harriet's best friend. If something was going on in Harriet's life that would have made her the target of the person to plant the bomb, she might know about it. I tried speaking to Helen early on, but it just seemed to make her mad. She seemed to think I was trying to push this whole thing onto Harriet and that I was accusing Harriet of doing something that led to her getting herself blown up. But that wasn't my intent at all. Well, not exactly. If Harriet did make a very nasty enemy and the bomb was placed in her purse as some sort of retaliation geared toward her, then everyone else who was injured that night was simply in the wrong place at the wrong time. I'm not trying to say that Lloyd's death and Hank's paralysis were Harriet's fault, but if the bomber did plant the bomb because of a problem he or she had with Harriet, we need to figure out what sort of trouble Harriet might have gotten herself into."

I knew that a conversation with Helen regarding Harriet's role in the bombing if indeed she had been the target, was not going to be an easy conversation to have. "I'll talk to her," I offered. "I have no idea what I am going to say, but I'll try."

Roy ran a hand through his hair. "Thank you. That would be helpful. If we don't get a break soon, I think this case is going to be the end of me."

"Kyle and I are here for you and willing to help in any way we can. Kyle and Jeff are working on getting the town council up and running which should help as well, although it will be awhile. I suppose there are those like James who will benefit from the chaos and those who will suffer negative consequences from that same chaos and delay."

Roy leaned back, a look of fatigue on his face. "I guess that rebuilding that which was lost is going to be an important next step." Roy glanced at Kyle. "I'm sorry that this whole thing has been dumped on you."

Kyle shrugged. "I'm happy to help in any way I can. Jeff and Tj are going to help out as well. The first course of action is going to be to get folks in place who can fill the openings left by Hank and Lloyd, as well as the open seat we already had."

"That makes sense. I'm sure you can use all the help you can get," Roy said.

Kyle nodded. "It's going to be a time-consuming job. Not only do we need three new council members, in addition to the mayor we already needed, but we also need a new town clerk/mayor's secretary and a new venue for the town hall as well."

"Seems like an overwhelming task," Roy shook his head slowly.

"Kyle and Jeff are making a list of potential town council members," I informed Roy. "Do you have any suggestions?"

Roy considered this for a moment and then responded. "How about Doc? He seems to have a lot of free time on his hands, he is intelligent, and he seems to approach situations in a fair and open-minded manner."

I glanced at Kyle. "Doc would be a good choice. I don't know if he'd want to do it, but it couldn't hurt to put him on the list."

"What about your dad?" Roy asked.

"He'd be fantastic," I answered, "but he is still recovering from the car accident he was involved in last summer, and he has the resort to run. Besides that, he is about to be married. I don't think he has the time to really commit to such a huge undertaking. Still, I don't suppose it would hurt to run it past him. I'd hate to make an assumption on his behalf that wasn't accurate."

"We've actually come up with a pretty strong list," Kyle said. "The question is: can we get three of the potential candidates to make the commitment."

Roy swallowed the last of his coffee. "I guess all you can really do is approach the task systematically and see where you end up."

After Roy left, Kyle and I decided to take a walk. While coming up with a strategy to rebuild the town council was important, I didn't want to lose sight of the need to find the person who killed our friends. We were both feeling better physically, so it was time to stop being cautious and jump in with both feet.

"In my mind, in terms of the bombing, now that we suspect the bomb was planted in Harriet's purse, we really need to look at the possibility that Harriet was the intended victim," Kyle suggested.

I felt my stomach begin to churn. "The idea that Harriet was the target makes the whole thing seem all that much more personal."

Kyle tightened his hand over mine. "It does feel personal, which I suppose is due to the fact that it is personal. I really can't imagine who would want not only to kill a sweet woman like Harriet but to kill her in such a violent manner." Kyle turned and looked at me. "I've known Harriet since I moved to Serenity, but I can't claim to have really *known* her. Who was she really? Where was she from? What did she do in her spare time? If she had enemies who might those enemies have been?"

I frowned. "All good questions. I've known Harriet my whole life, but I can't say that I know where she was born or anything about her family. I don't even know for certain when she moved to Serenity. I do know that she has been a fixture at the town hall ever since I can remember. She was strong-willed and opinionated, and she wasn't afraid to be vocal about her opinions. Everyone who knew her knew she was a huge gossip. She had a lot of friends in the community, but I remember her being best friends with Helen since I was a kid. Even though she could seem brash at times, I think she really cared about people. In terms of what she did with her off time, I know she did a lot of volunteer work, and she spent a significant amount of time hanging out with both Helen and Frannie. As far as I know, she never married nor had children. If she had parents, siblings, or other relatives still living, I don't remember ever meeting them. Roy was right when he said that if there were anyone who knew the real Harriet Kramer, it would be Helen. I just hope I can find a way to bring up the subject without causing the poor woman more pain and suffering than she has already been forced to endure."

"Maybe you should start with Frannie," Kyle suggested. "She may not have been as close to Harriet as Helen, but the two women were good friends. They have both lived in Serenity for a very long time, and they were close to the same age. She may know more than you think."

I laid my head on Kyle's shoulder. "Yeah, that is actually a good idea. I will start with Frannie. I'm sure Frannie is grieving Harriet's death the same as Helen, but her husband didn't almost die in the same explosion, so I would assume she is handling the whole thing better. She might even be able to tell us what we need to know without bothering Helen. I need to talk with her about Thanksgiving anyway."

"Thanksgiving?" Kyle asked.

"Rosalie ran into her in town. Frannie usually comes out to the resort for Thanksgiving dinner and asked Rosalie about it. Rosalie told her that we were hosting this year but that she was sure she was invited. I just want to confirm this fact with

Frannie personally."

"So far, I have only mentioned it to my mom, who plans to attend with Annabeth and Kiara." Annabeth and Kiara Boswell were sisters who Kyle decided to help out after their father was sent to prison. Kyle paid for Kiara to attend college, and Annabeth, who was currently sixteen, had been living with Kyle's mother and attending the local high school. "I guess we should make a list, so we are sure to speak to everyone we need to. I'd hate for anyone to be left out."

"That's a good idea. We can do it later. The library is open until two on Saturday so we should go now if we don't want to miss her."

# CHAPTER 10

Frannie Edison worked as the librarian for the Serenity Library, which was one of my favorite places in town. Originally built as a bordello at the turn of the century, it had been converted into a library more than sixty years earlier, a few years after the town was incorporated. The downstairs, which at one time had served as a common room for entertaining, now held a large wooden counter that was used as a reference desk but had originally served as the bar on which girls had danced to entertain the men. Behind the counter were rows of bookshelves that held reference materials that could only be accessed with librarian supervision. There was an open area in front of the counter where round tables surrounded by chairs were provided for patrons. The upstairs was divided into smaller rooms, converted from bedrooms into bookrooms, each with its own subject matter. One room was decorated in nursery rhymes and held children's books, another housed fiction, yet another was filled with reference and business books, and another held a selection of books on self-help and religion. Each bookroom contained long sofas or cozy chairs for visitors who wished to preview a book before checking it out and taking it home.

"Good afternoon, Frannie," I greeted after Kyle and I entered the building.

"Tj; Kyle. How nice to see you."

"Before I forget I wanted to let you know that Kyle and I are hosting Thanksgiving at his place this year, and as always, both you and Hazel are invited." I referred to Hazel Whipple, the town's postmistress, who didn't drive and usually came to Thanksgiving dinner with Frannie.

Frannie smiled. "Thank you, I'd like that very much, and I know that Hazel will as well. And I'm happy to see that you both seem to have recovered from the explosion."

My smile faded a bit. "Yes, Kyle and I are doing much better. We are sad about Harriet and Lloyd."

I couldn't help but notice that Frannie's eyes teared up just a bit. "I'm still having such a hard time with the idea that I'll never see Harriet again. It seems like a horrible dream that I keep hoping I'll awaken from." Fannie used the back of her hand to wipe her eyes. "Have you heard if Roy has figured out who did this terrible thing?"

"We spoke to him this morning, and he still wasn't sure," I answered. "But he did say that it looks as if the bomb was hidden inside that big old purse Harriet carried everywhere she went. The bomb had been set up on a timer, and if not for the last-minute meeting, Harriet would likely have been home alone. He is looking into the possibility that she was the intended target rather than an individual member of the council or the council as a whole."

The color drained from Frannie's face. "Oh my." She slid into the chair behind her. "I hadn't heard that the bomb was in Harriet's purse. I guess I just assumed it had been hidden somewhere in the building." Frannie put a hand to her mouth. She looked as if she was going to be sick.

"Are you okay?" I asked, putting a hand on Frannie's arm.

"No. I don't think that I am. If not for the emergency town meeting, the two of us would have been together. Harriet planned to come here to the library to help me hand out candy as part of the town's Safe Halloween campaign."

I felt the blood drain from my own face. "So the library would have been full of kids."

Frannie nodded. "Kids and their parents."

I knew the Safe Halloween idea had come about as an alternative for parents who didn't want to take their young children into neighborhoods where older teens occasionally created an unsafe environment. The Safe Halloween route was laid out along Main where the businesses and public agencies such as the library and post office agreed to stay open and hand out candy. If Harriet and the bomb in her purse had been inside the busy library when it went off, I hated to think of the human causalities that could have occurred.

Kyle narrowed his gaze. "You don't think that someone intended to blow up a bunch of kids, do you?"

"I don't know. I hope not." I looked at Frannie. "Do you know who might have known that Harriet planned to be here?"

Frannie shook her head. "I don't know. Maybe no one. I really don't know why Harriet would mention her plans to anyone unless they asked. On any other Tuesday night, she would most likely have been home alone. Thursday is book club, and we try to grab a meal together on Friday's. Sometimes we go shopping or take in a movie on the weekends, but Mondays and Tuesdays are usually nights devoted to catching up on paperwork for both of us. She has her shows on Hallmark, and I have my shows on The History Channel. We normally make an easy dinner, turn on our shows, and do our paperwork." Frannie looked at me. "I need to call Helen."

"Helen? Why?"

"If Harriet was the intended victim, I might know why."

"You do? Why?"

"I can't say. At least not yet. I need to call Helen."

I took a step back. "Okay. Go ahead and call Helen and then we'll talk."

Frannie went into her office while Kyle and I waited by the front counter. After a good ten minutes, she finally came out. "Helen is willing to hear what you have to say. She doesn't want to leave Bookman, and wondered if we could come to her place."

"Sure, we can do that. Should we call Roy?"

"Not yet. Helen has some questions before we go any further."

I glanced at Kyle. He nodded.

"Okay," I said. "Let's go and talk to Helen."

Frannie decided to follow us in her own car, leaving Kyle and I free to talk on the ride to Bookman's mansion. "What do you think that was all about?" I asked.

"I don't know, but it seems obvious that Frannie, and probably Helen, know something about Harriet. Something that wouldn't come into play if the bomb was planted to blow up the town hall or the town council members, but does come into play if Harriet herself was the intended victim."

"Helen was Harriet's best friend. She isn't going to want to reveal her secrets if she doesn't have to."

"Which is probably why she wanted to ask questions before we bring Roy into this," Kyle pointed out. "It is likely that neither Frannie nor Helen considered the fact that Harriet might have been the intended victim all along. I'm sure they will need time to process this new information."

Kyle was right. Helen seemed to have her shield up from the moment we walked in the front door. I knew that it was important at this point to tread lightly. I greeted the woman as I took off my coat, making sure to ask about Bookman. Helen assured us that Bookman was doing better and would be joining us for our discussion. That was fine with me. Bookman tended to have a calming effect on Helen, and if things got dicey, I was sure his steady influence would be welcome.

"So what is this about Harriet being the intended victim?"

Helen asked as soon as we'd all gathered around the dining table. I was happy to see that Bookman, while extremely pale, was able to sit with us in relative comfort.

"Based on a conversation we had with Roy, it looks as if the bomb that killed both Harriet and Lloyd may have been placed inside Harriet's purse at some point prior to the town council meeting," I began. "We don't know when it was placed in her purse if that is what actually occurred, but we do assume that Harriet didn't know it was there. Up to this point, we haven't been certain whether the town council was the target or Harriet was the target, but given the tight timeline between the meeting being called at five o'clock and Harriet placing her purse in the drawer at the town hall at around five forty-five, it seems reasonable that we can eliminate the town council as the intended victim."

"How do you know when the meeting was called and when Harriet put her purse in her drawer?" Helen asked.

"I spoke to Jeff," I answered. "Jeff told me that he received the text about the emergency meeting at around five o'clock just as he was closing up his shop for the day. That fits with the time that Kyle received the same text. After receiving the text, Jeff headed directly to the town hall. When he arrived, Lloyd was already there. Bookman came in shortly after, and at about five forty-five, give or take a few minutes, Harriet came into the council chambers from her office carrying that huge purse she always carries around. Jeff told me that Hank came in shortly after Harriet, and of course, Kyle and I were late and didn't arrive until seconds before the bomb exploded at six."

Helen looked at Bookman.

"My memory is still pretty fuzzy, but that seems right," he confirmed.

"If the bomb was in Harriet's purse, wouldn't she have realized it was there?" Helen asked.

"Perhaps, but it is possible that the bomb had been slipped into her purse and she hadn't noticed. Roy shared with me the fact that the bomb was about the size of a softball and weighed less than five pounds. An extremely powerful explosive was used, so we know this was no amateur job. Someone with munitions experience had to have built the device."

"It just seems that if a five-pound object was placed in Harriet's purse, she would have noticed the minute she picked up the purse," Helen insisted. "Maybe you are wrong about the bomb being in her purse."

Frannie gave Helen a look that seemed to be an attempt to encourage her to tell what she knew, but she shook her head and then turned away. I knew I needed to let Helen take the time she needed to tell us what Frannie was ready to tell.

I looked at Helen and offered her what I hoped was a sincere look of sympathy. "We don't know with a hundred percent certainty that the bomb was in Harriet's purse but based on the evidence the crime scene guys turned up, it does look that way. Add in the tight timeline, and it seems likely, but I do understand what you are saying about Harriet noticing the change in weight. Maybe Harriet did know the bomb was in her purse, but maybe it was disguised as something else."

"Like what?" Helen asked a frown on her face.

I shrugged. "I don't know. Maybe it was wrapped. Maybe someone gave her a gift with instructions to open it later. Or maybe she was given a wrapped package and asked to give it to someone else she planned to see later in the day or in the week. We can't really know at this point, but I don't think we should assume that it wouldn't be possible for Helen to have agreed to transport the bomb without knowing that it was a bomb."

I glanced at Bookman, who was frowning but hadn't said anything else. Helen was as white as a sheet, and Frannie looked as if she was going to pass out at any moment. "I know this is hard on both of you," I said. "But with the timeline between Harriet calling the meeting at five and the bomb going off at six, it really does seem as if the bomb was already in Harriet's purse before the meeting was even called. Frannie told me that Harriet would have been home at six on a normal Tuesday, but the Tuesday in question was Halloween and she planned to attend the event being held at the library. In my mind, that means that either Harriet was the intended victim or the event was the intended victim. We need to figure out which." I couldn't help but notice that Frannie glanced at Helen, who narrowed her gaze. I glanced at Kyle and Bookman. "I'd like to speak to Helen and Frannie alone."

Both men agreed and retreated to the other room. I hated to see Bookman so frail, but I was happy to see that he seemed to be on the road to recovery.

"I know your instinct is to protect your friend," I began once the men had exited the room, "but if Harriet was the intended victim, then knowing what was going on in her life is going to be the key to finding her killer." I looked at Frannie. "When we spoke in the library, you indicated that if Harriet was the intended victim, you might know why. I need you to tell me what you know."

Frannie looked at Helen, who looked as if she was going to refuse to cooperate, but eventually, Helen began to speak. "Something was going on with Harriet that might have gotten her killed. She had a really tough time dealing with Mayor Harper's death, which is understandable since not only had the two been friends for decades but after Judge Harper took on the role of mayor, they worked long hours side by side to get the town back on track after Mayor Wallaby destroyed confidence in the town council and the role of mayor."

Helen paused. She glanced at Frannie, who continued on her behalf.

"Initially, Helen and I tried to be understanding and supportive of Harriet's odd mood and somewhat erratic behavior. While it was true that the entire town was in shock after the accident which killed Mayor Harper and put your dad in the hospital, we knew that Harriet was closer to him than most, and therefore it was natural that his death seemed to hit her the hardest. We hoped that time would heal her grief, but as time went by, instead of working through her grief, she seemed to channel that energy into anger."

"Anger?" I asked.

"When she found out that the events leading up to Mayor Harper's death were the result of a secret he'd kept, she became fixated on secrets as being the root of all evil," Frannie provided.

Helen jumped in. "That might be a grandiose statement for what was going on, but while Frannie and I were unaware of it at the time, at some point, Harriet decided to channel her natural inclination to gossip into a brand new hobby that both Frannie and I tried to talk her out of once we finally realized what was really happening."

I frowned as I tried to understand what the women were trying to communicate to me. "New hobby?" It was true that Harriet had always been the number two source for the latest gossip, second only to Helen. Of course, once Helen married Bookman, and she was no longer hanging out at The Antiquery all day, Harriet had pretty much moved into the number one position.

"In the past, Harriet liked to gossip, but it was all pretty harmless," Frannie said.

"But then, Mayor Harper died, and Harriet's gossiping began to take on a policing quality," Helen added.

My eyes grew wide, and I gasped. "Harriet was the author of Sinful Secrets."

Helen nodded.

Sinful Secrets was a blog that had shown up in email boxes around town beginning in late July. The blog was a gossip rag that focused on revealing the secrets of anyone and everyone the author of the blog chose to pick on. The blog had started with the tone of any other gossip rag, but as time went by, the content of the blog had become downright mean. As a motive for murder, the blog fit the bill perfectly.

"But the August issue of that blog seemed to be a direct hit at you," I reminded Helen. "The three secrets revealed were: the plot and working title of the book Bookman had just completed and wanted to keep secret until the big reveal party, the fact that Bree had been locking lips with Pastor Dan in spite of the fact that she had also been working as his nanny, and the fact that Jenna and Dennis had been having marital problems since his promotion to Captain. Why would Harriet pick on the people you loved the most? She was your best friend."

Helen blew out a shallow breath. "I don't know why she decided to write what she did. At the time the blog came out, I was livid that someone would pick on my family that way. Keep in mind, I didn't know that Harriet was behind the whole thing at that point, and the two of us even talked about how mean and inappropriate the person behind the blog was, and how they needed to be punished. Harriet even made a comment about the person being a coward since she was clearly hiding behind her anonymity. When I finally found out that Harriet had been writing the blog all along, I wanted to wring her neck. I confronted her and asked her about her motive for being so evil and she reminded me that I had been the queen of gossip in the area for decades and that the secrets she had revealed about Bookman's book, Bree's relationship with Dan, and Jenna's marital problems were really no worse than the sort of things I had whispered into the ears of town residents for years before marrying Bookman and retiring from the gossip game."

"But Bookman is your husband, and Jenna and Bree are your daughters. How could she do that to you or to them?"

Helen bowed her head. "I don't know. Of course, I was very upset about what she had done, but the fact that she knew about the plot and title of Bookman's book, Bree and Dan's relationship, and Jenna and Dennis's marital problems was because I'd told her. It really was my own gossiping that came back to bite me. Harriet and I were never close after I found out what she had been doing, but she didn't deserve to die."

"That may be true, but not all the secrets revealed by the Sinful Secrets blog were harmless," I pointed out. "The blog is responsible for Nancy Johnson filing for divorce after Sinful Secrets revealed that her husband, Jimmy, had been seen heading into a motel room with an unidentified woman with long blond hair."

Helen cringed. Both she and Frannie looked as guilty as if they had written the blog themselves.

"The blog not only caused Jenna all sorts of grief with Dennis, but I know of at least two other relationships that were destroyed by what was revealed," I continued. "Why didn't you tell someone what Harriet was doing? The person behind that horrible blog has been the biggest mystery to hit the town of Serenity in decades."

"We didn't know until recently," Frannie said.

Helen nodded. "When the first blog came out in July, it was light-hearted and funny. Sure, it picked on some of the town's favorite citizens including you and Kyle, and it made a few folks mad, but all in all, it seemed that most of the town's residents found the blog to be entertaining. Then the second blog came out at the end of August, and it was focused on my family. And yes, I was angry. Livid in fact. But I didn't know who was writing the blog, and it didn't seem that enough harm had been done to spend a lot of time trying to figure it out. Then when the

September blog came out, and Jimmy's affair was revealed, along with a few other gasp-worthy revelations about other folks in town, I could see the opinion of many folks in town begin to change. There were those who felt that the blog was causing more harm than it ought to, and perhaps the blogger should be stopped. I found I agreed and I even made noise about tracking down whoever was responsible and making them pay, but I had no idea who the blogger was or how to track down the identity of this very hurtful person."

Frannie continued after Helen paused. "Then the October blog came out, and the author of Sinful Secrets revealed that Margie Holden's husband, Carl, was not, in fact, the father of their middle daughter, but that she had been conceived during a brief affair between Margie and her tennis instructor. No one knew Margie's secret except for Helen, who Margie had confided in."

"I unwisely shared this information with Harriet after a girls' night out, and the next week, Margie's secret was revealed in the blog." Helen bowed her head. "Of course, not only were both Margie and her husband hurt by this bit of news being made public, but Margie's seven-year-old daughter found out that Carl was not her father, as did her classmates, and the fallout nearly destroyed the young girl. It was then that I figured out that Harriet was the author of the blog. I confronted her, and she promised to stop publishing it. The damage from the blogs she had already published could not be undone, and she promised not to write any new ones, so I didn't see the value in ratting her out, even though I knew our relationship had been damaged beyond repair." Helen wiped a tear from her cheek. "Perhaps if I had ratted her out, she'd be alive today. Perhaps Lloyd wouldn't be dead, Hank wouldn't be crippled, and Bookman wouldn't have almost died." Helen glanced at me. "I'm sorry. This whole thing is my fault."

"It's not your fault. I probably wouldn't have said anything either once Harriet promised to stop what she was doing. I still can't believe that Harriet would do such a hurtful thing."

"I don't think she meant it to be hurtful," Frannie said. "At least not in the beginning. I think that she honestly believed after Mayor Harper died as a result of his secret, that secrets were dangerous, and the telling of them could very well save lives."

"I think Harper's death messed with Harriet's mind more than any of us really understood. If I had to guess, she sort of lost it after his death, but since she seemed to be dealing with things, at least on the surface, no one really knew how it had affected her," Helen added.

"I don't blame either of you. I even sort of understand why Harriet might have felt justified in doing what she did, but now that I know about the blog, Harriet as the target of the bomb makes sense. Why didn't you bring this up before?"

Harriet and Frannie glanced at each other. Neither spoke at first, but eventually, Helen replied. "As far we know, Frannie and I are the only two who know that Harriet was behind the Sinful Secrets blog. We knew we didn't plant the bomb, so we didn't think the blog was the motive. In fact, until today, we just assumed that the council as a whole was the target and the motive was something the council was working on."

I supposed I could understand that. I hadn't suspected that Harriet was the intended target until today either, and I'd been digging around in the incident. "I marked the blog as spam after the first one, and never even read any of them after that, although I have heard quite a bit about the content from those affected, especially Jenna. Still, I think reading what was said could be important. Do you have copies?"

Both Helen and Frannie admitted that they didn't, but they suspected that the blogs were saved on Harriet's home computer.

"I'll call Roy and see if he has her computer. In the meantime, the two of you need to keep this conversation between us. If someone from the blog did plant the bomb in Harriet's purse, I don't want them getting wind that we are onto them which would give them the opportunity to disappear before Roy can identify and arrest them."

# CHAPTER 11

After the meeting, Kyle and I headed to his place. I called Roy, who headed to Harriet's to get her computer. At this point, it seemed to me that the key to finding the killer was to identify those individuals who'd been injured by Harriet's tell-all blogs.

"I'm still having a hard time coming to grips with the fact that Harriet is the person behind the blogs," Kyle said as he made a pot of coffee.

"I only read the first one which included a comment about you and me locking lips, and a comment about Rita Halliwell having a temper and slapping the new flower delivery guy when he tried to make a move on her. There was also something about Mark Riverton being a secret hoarder who'd kept everything he had ever owned. The blog was written in a lighthearted tone that wasn't really cruel, but it did seem like the author was just trying to stir things up, so I marked the blog as spam and any additional blogs sent to my email would have ended up in my spam folder." I frowned. "I wonder if they are still there."

"Do you delete your spam?"

"Not very often. I have my laptop, I'll take a look."

Unfortunately, the only blog in my spam folder was the most recent blog, which was sent out in October, but it was a place to start.

"Read me what it says, and I'll jot down the names of those

affected," Kyle suggested as we settled in at the kitchen table with our coffee.

The blog contained just three paragraphs. There wasn't a lot of text in any of the paragraphs, but there was enough to cause a lot of damage. I began to read. "Sinful secrets can easily turn into sinful lies when matters of the heart are at stake, and sinful lies, as we all know, can lead to all sorts of unforeseen tragedy. It was discovered this week by Sinful Secrets that for the past two months, Brandy Baldwin's Monday night book club has really been Brandy Baldwin's Monday night booty call. Reliable sources have confirmed that Brandy's husband, Walter, has been biding his time at home with the twins while Brandy has been getting a little something on the side from local boy-toy, Ryder Walton." I glanced at Kyle. "Ouch. That is downright mean."

Kyle nodded. "I agree. This blog doesn't have the same lighthearted and funny tone as the first blog in July. Whether this is true or not, I can see both Brandy and Walter as having the motive to want revenge against the blogger who filled the entire town in on their marital woes."

"What about Ryder?" I asked.

"Ryder is single and proud of the fact that he gets around. If I had to guess, he was thrilled that everyone knew that he'd managed to bag a good-looking woman like Brandy."

I raised a brow. "Bag?"

"I'm sorry. That was rude. But you know what I mean?"

I nodded. "I do."

Kyle wrote Walter and Brandy Baldwin down on his list. "What's next?"

I looked down at the blog and continued to read. "It seems that lust has run wild in Serenity, both currently and in the past, and Sinful Secrets is here to reveal it all. With a tiny bit of research into classified records, it has been confirmed by Sinful

Secrets that Serenity's most respectable housewife and mother has been keeping a shameful secret of her own involving the real father of her middle daughter, Haley, who Sinful Secrets has discovered, does not belong to her husband, the tireless, Carl Holden." I glanced up at Kyle. "I can't believe Harriet wrote this. Even if she was grieving, even if she went a little bit over the edge with Harper's death, this whole thing is just so mean."

Kyle bobbed his head. "Yeah. It's pretty bad. You said there were three paragraphs?"

I looked back at my computer and began to read the third paragraph. "And finally, when it comes to lustful thoughts and deeds, it seems worth mentioning that Sinful Secrets has uncovered the fact that our own Hank Hammond was seen grinding pelvises with the newest waitress at The Beef and Brew, Fiona Walton, who by the way, is barely out of her teens and almost two decades younger than our esteemed restauranteur and town council member."

Kyle frowned. "Why on earth would Harriet print that? First of all, Hank is single, and it isn't really a scandal for him to have intimate relations with whomever he wants, and it appeared to me that Harriet really liked Hank. I never saw any indication that she was out to get him."

"Helen was her best friend, and she devoted the entire August blog to tell-all posts relating to her husband and daughters."

"True."

"Helen didn't seem to think that Harriet's intent was evil, at least not at first. She said that it was her opinion that Harriet actually believed she was keeping those with secrets from future harm by revealing their secrets before the secret led them to harm. Of course, that reasoning is crazy, but I'm beginning to think that perhaps, in the end, Harriet really had gone over the edge." I glanced at Kyle's list. "While we have some viable suspects from the October blog and we know the content of the July and August blogs, we do need to get ahold of the September blog. If they aren't on Harriet's computer, I'll see if I can find someone who saved them."

"So Helen really didn't realize that Harriet was the author of Sinful Secrets until the October blog published?" Kyle asked with a look of doubt on his face.

"Not according to what she told me. She said that Harriet never said or did anything to indicate she was behind the blogs, and it wasn't until Helen realized that Harriet was one of the few people who knew about the secret behind Haley Baldwin's birth that she began to suspect that Harriet was involved."

By the time Kyle and I had made our primary list, Roy arrived with the computer. It was password protected, so Kyle got to work breaking the passcode while Roy and I chatted.

"I managed to track down the four blogs which had already been published," Roy said.

"I read the first one, and I know the content of the second one, which featured Bookman, Bree, and Jenna. I had the most recent blog in my spam folder, but we still need to take a look at September."

Roy used his tablet to pull up the missing blog. By the time the September issue of Sinful Secrets was published, Harriet had definitely passed over to the dark side. The September blog had the information about Jimmy cheating on Nancy, as well as proof that Adam Levine had likewise been cheating on his wife, Veronica. A statement was also made about Wilma Fisher embezzling funds from her boss, which resulted in her being fired and criminal charges being brought against her. After deleting victims such as Kyle and me, Jenna and Dennis, Bookman, and Bree and Pastor Dan, we ended up with ten suspects: Nancy and Jimmy Johnson, Walter and Brandy Baldwin, Margie and Carl Holden, Adam and Veronica Levine,

Mark Riverton and Wilma Fisher.

"I'll talk to all of them, and we'll see where we end up," Roy said. He looked at Kyle. "You should still try to get into her computer. It has occurred to me that Harriet might have other victims lined up to rat out. She has presented just three victims per month at this point. I can see how she might have other revelations just waiting for an opening. I can also see that someone might have figured out what she was doing and killed her to keep her quiet. I know Helen said Harriet promised to stop publishing the blog, but that doesn't mean she would have. And even if she wasn't going to publish it, potential victims who may have found out what she planned to reveal may not have known she planned to retire."

"I'll get in," Kyle promised. "I'll call you when I do."

After Roy left, it occurred to me that perhaps it might be worth our while to search Harriet's home. I was sure that Roy and/or his partner, Kate, had already done so, but I knew I would feel better if I took a peek myself. Kyle wasn't a fan of breaking into her home since it was right smack dab in the middle of a neighborhood with a bunch of close neighbors, but I knew Helen had a key, so I asked if we could use it, and when she agreed, Kyle and I picked it up and then headed toward Harriet's.

"I've been inside this home dozens of times," I said to Kyle after we arrived, "but now that I know Harriet is dead, the place feels somewhat creepy and haunted."

"I doubt the house is haunted, but I do understand what you mean. Let's start with her home office and see what we can find. I'm hoping my software will have broken the password on Harriet's computer by the time we get home. Between what we find here and what we find on the computer, I'm hoping we will have an idea as to the identity of our killer by the end of the day."

"That would be nice."

I followed Kyle through the living room and down the hallway to Harriet's office. The first thing I noticed was that the room had been tossed. The file cabinet drawers were open, and every file that had been stored within was on the floor.

"I think someone beat us to it," Kyle said.

"You don't think the cops did this?"

Kyle shook his head. "No. If they searched the place, they would have been a lot more deliberate in their effort. If I had to guess, the person who killed Harriet was most likely the one to come by looking for something. Don't touch anything. We should call Roy. He might be able to find some prints or other physical evidence."

After calling Roy, Kyle and I headed back to his place. This investigation seemed to be getting increasingly frustrating with every clue we uncovered.

"Grandpa planned to head over to Doc's to work on the investigation into the explosion. Doc is a pretty smart cookie, perhaps we should call them and see what, if anything, they might have figured out," I suggested.

"Sounds fine with me. Ask them to come over if you want."

I called Grandpa, and he informed me that they did have news to share and would be right over. I made yet another pot of coffee and set out some snacks. All this running around was exhausting, in spite of the fact it was only mid-afternoon.

By the time Doc's car pulled up in the driveway, the coffee had brewed. "So you said you had news?" I asked Grandpa after he and Doc had settled around the dining table with Kyle and me.

Grandpa looked at Doc. "Doc knows a guy who knows a guy who was owed a favor by one of the men who works at the crime lab." Doc used to be a coroner, so more often than not, he had connections when we needed them the most. "According to the contact working the case, the bomb that was used to blow up the town hall was military grade stuff and not something an amateur might throw together."

"So are you saying that someone in the military is behind this?"

"Not at all," Doc answered my query. "The bomb was military grade, but it is also a munition that is readily available on the black market for the right price."

"So our killer has money," Kyle said.

Doc nodded. "Money and influence. This made me think about James Kingston."

"Roy said he spoke to James, and he didn't think he was behind this," I responded. "Besides, we have new information to share about Harriet's role in the whole thing."

I filled Grandpa and Doc in on everything we had learned from Roy, as well as from Frannie and Helen. To say that both Doc and Grandpa were shocked would be putting it mildly.

"I just can't imagine Harriet doing such a thing," Grandpa said, shaking his head. "I've known Harriet since before you were born. She did tend to gossip, and she occasionally took a rigid stance when it came to what she considered to be appropriate versus inappropriate behavior, but I've never known her to be intentionally hurtful."

I offered Grandpa a look of compassion. "I was surprised as well, but after everything that Helen told me, it sort of fits."

"Did any of the victims of her blog have the connections or financial resources to buy a bomb on the black market?" Doc asked.

Kyle and I went through each of the suspects we had identified one at a time. After discussing possible means of obtaining the cash they'd need to buy a military grade bomb, we came to the conclusion that it was highly unlikely that any of the ten were the killer we were after.

"Harriet's home office was tossed," I said. "This leads me to believe that someone was after something that hasn't been made public yet."

"Maybe one of the subjects of the November blog had reason to suspect that Helen was the one behind the blog, and decided to stop her," Grandpa suggested.

I nodded. "That makes as much sense as anything."

"Has anyone been able to get a peek at the November blog?" Doc asked. "It seems that Harriet might have started to work on it."

"Kyle is working on it, but so far, we haven't come across any files associated with the blog," I answered.

"I'll find them," Kyle promised. "If the files exist, and I suspect they do, I'll find them."

Doc frowned as he sat back in his chair. "If the theory is that someone gave something to Harriet, such as a wrapped gift to open later or to pass on to someone else, they must have been by the town offices on the day of the bombing. Harriet wouldn't put the gift in her purse and then carry it around for days, but I can see her putting the gift in her purse and then taking it home or dropping it off with the person for whom it was intended."

"So the killer had to have been in Harriet's office on the day of the bombing," I said.

Doc nodded. "That does make sense. I know the town office, like the council chambers, was destroyed in the blast, but the town hall did have video surveillance. The video from that day must be saved in the cloud somewhere."

Kyle jumped up. "Of course. Why didn't I think of that?" He hurried across the room and picked up his laptop. He brought it back to the table and logged on. It took him a few minutes to find what he was looking for. He frowned.

"What is it?" I asked.

"The security video from that day has been deleted. The

system was turned off once the file was deleted. The last video in the cloud is of the day prior to the bombing."

"Deleted? Who has access?" I asked.

"Bookman, Harriet, myself, as well as the security company the town contracts with." Kyle looked up from his screen. "It is much more likely that the site was hacked than it is that someone with access deleted the video feed."

"So our killer is someone with both the connections and financial wherewithal to buy a military grade explosive, and the skill to hack into the town's security system and delete an entire file?" I asked.

Kyle nodded. "It looks like that might be the case."

Well, that can't be good.

Kyle and I chatted with Doc and Grandpa for a while longer. We discussed possible suspects who might be connected, wealthy, and have computer skills that would allow them to hack into the town's security system, but in the end, we didn't come up with anyone. We all agreed that we would continue to ponder the question in the hope that something would eventually come to one of us. After Doc and Grandpa left, I turned to Kyle. "I told Jenna I would meet her for a drink this afternoon, and then I thought I'd talk to the girls about our engagement. Is that okay?"

Kyle looked surprised by my question. "Of course. You don't have to ask me for permission to spend time with your best friend or chat with your sisters."

"I know. I just feel like I am deserting you."

"I'm fine. Really. I think I am going to work on the files I've been able to download from the town's server. Finding the person who killed Lloyd and Harriet is important, but putting a band-aid on the town is important as well. At some point, I feel like everything is going to come crashing down if we don't start to put things back together sooner than later."

I began gathering my belongings. It had been such a long day. Was it really just this morning that I had told Jenna about Kyle and me? It seemed so long ago. I had meant to tell Kyle right away that I had shared our news with Jenna, but I guess with everything that was going on, I hadn't gotten around to it. "I told Jenna about us getting married. I know we decided to wait to tell anyone, but she picked up on something I said, and it sort of slipped out."

Kyle smiled softly. "I'm fine with you telling anyone you want, whenever you want."

"I've been thinking about things, and I think I should tell Ashley and Gracie before I tell anyone else."

"Sure. I understand that."

"After I tell them, I think I should tell my dad and grandpa. They deserve to know before we tell people in general. Oh and your mother too, of course."

Kyle stepped forward and wrapped his arms around my waist. "I agree with all of that, especially that Ashley and Gracie should be told first. Our marrying affects them almost as much as it affects us. Should we tell them together?"

I took a step back. "I think it might be best if I talk to Ashley and Gracie alone. At least initially. I want them to feel free to express any concerns they may have, and I know that if you are part of the conversation, Gracie might not express what is on her mind. She loves you, and she wouldn't want to hurt your feelings even if she does have questions or concerns."

Kyle nodded. "Yeah. Okay. I guess that makes sense. I suppose I should have considered the fact that the girls might not be happy about our decision."

"You know they love you."

"I know, but our getting married will be a big change for them. You are right to be concerned about how they will take the news."

No wonder I loved this man. He always put the needs of others before his own. "I'll talk to them tonight. Once I feel that they have had the chance to speak their minds, we can talk to them together."

# CHAPTER 12

Drinks with Jenna turned into wine at her kitchen table once we realized that Dennis had a shift and there was no one to watch the girls who'd all congregated at her house once she'd returned from sitting with Bookman that morning. It was nice to spend time with her, but I could see that she was exhausted, so our visit was short, although she did have some good advice for my conversation with Ashley and Gracie: Keep it real, validate their feelings and concerns whatever they might be, but tell the truth, and don't, at any point, try to downplay my intention to marry Kyle with or without their permission. Jenna was right. Ashley had a tendency to be manipulative, and I had a tendency to get drawn into her manipulation. If I entered the conversation from the position of asking for their permission to marry Kyle, things were bound to disintegrate to the point where I'd find myself promising to put our wedding on the back burner. I needed to let them know I *was* marrying Kyle but wanted to be sure their questions were answered and their concerns addressed.

"So did you girls have fun today?" I asked after the three of us congregated on Gracie's bed along with her dog, Pumpkin, and cat, Crissy.

"So much fun," Ashley said. "Rosalie can sew really well. The purses she helped Kristi and me make are going to make all the girls in our class so jealous. After Jenna picked us up, she took us to the store with her, and everyone was looking at them and commenting on how awesome they were."

"It is a pretty great purse. It looks like you are really getting into sewing."

Ashley grinned. "I love it. Kristi does too, although Jenna can sew, so Kristi has help at home. I know you don't like to sew, but now that Papa is marrying Rosalie and she is living with us full time, I'll have help any time I want. Rosalie said she'd talk to Papa about turning one of the guest rooms into a sewing room where we can each have our own sewing machine and sewing closet."

I forced a smile. "That sounds really great." Dang it. How I was I going to convince Ashley that moving out to Kyle's was going to be a good idea when Rosalie was dangling a sewing room over her head? Of course, Rosalie didn't know I planned to move in with Kyle, and she was doing a nice thing for Ashley, so I supposed it would be petty of me to be mad. I looked at Gracie. "How was the movie with Papa?"

"It was fun. I love princess movies, and Papa bought us whatever we wanted from the snack bar instead of making us share like you usually do. Kari ate a whole tub of popcorn and drank a large soda by herself. I think it made her tummy rumbly, but it was fun to be able to each choose our own things."

"I bet it was. Did you get your costume for the play?"

Gracie nodded. "Kari didn't want to be a tree, so Papa talked Ms. Woods into letting her be an Indian girl."

"That's wonderful. It sounds like you both had an awesome day."

Gracie picked up Crissy who had crawled into her lap. She gave the soft gray cat a gentle hug. "We did. Did you have a fun day too?"

"I did," I lied since the day had turned out to be anything but fun.

"How is Kyle feeling?" Gracie asked. "Are his ribs better?"

"They are getting better, but you still can't jump on him when you see him. I thought that maybe the two of you could come out to dinner with Kyle and me tomorrow."

Ashley shrugged. "I guess."

"Can we get pizza?" Gracie asked.

"Anything you want."

"I want lobster," Ashley said. "Pizza is for babies."

Trying to stay away from things that were for babies was a big theme with Ashley lately, which only confirmed that she was ready to leave her childhood behind, and move onto the terrible teens.

"The last time I went to Rob's Pizza, half the place was filled with teenagers, so I don't think that pizza is for babies, but I wouldn't mind the four of us having a really nice dinner." I looked at Gracie. "I think The Beef and Brew is still closed, but there is that new steakhouse on the lake. They have lobster, which Ashley wants, but I think they have a casual dining menu as well. I don't know if they have pizza, but I'm sure they would have something that you would want. Would that be okay with you?"

Gracie frowned. "Can I wear the new dress Rosalie bought me?"

"Sure. That would be perfect for the restaurant."

Gracie crossed her legs under her body. "Okay."

*Okay, Tj, time to go in strong and direct.* "I do have something sort of important to talk to you about." I tried to keep the hesitation out of my voice, but I didn't sound as calm and casual as I'd hoped.

"Something bad?" Ashley asked.

I shook my head and forced a smile. "No. Something good. Very good."

"Are we getting a new puppy?" Gracie squealed.

"No, we aren't getting a new puppy. We have plenty of

animals. But it does involve an addition to the family."

"You're pregnant," Ashley accused.

"What? No, I'm not pregnant." Come on, girl pull it together. Honest and direct, I reminded myself to remember Jenna's advice. "Kyle and I are getting married."

My announcement was met with dead silence.

Eventually, Gracie spoke. "Married? When?"

"We just got engaged and haven't set a date, but it won't be for a while. Maybe next summer."

Gracie looked confused but not angry. I couldn't help but notice that Ashley had curled into a ball totally blocking me out.

"Is Kyle going to move in here with us when you get married?" Gracie asked.

"No dummy, Kyle isn't going to move in with us, Tj is going to make us move in with him," Ashley spat.

Gracie teared up. "But what about Papa? And Grandpa? What about Pumpkin and Crissy?"

I took a deep breath and let it out slowly. "Pumpkin and Crissy will move with us out to Kyle's place. Snowball too," I referred to Ashley's cat. "And we'll still see Papa and Grandpa all the time. As often as you want."

"Will Grandpa still make us breakfast?" Gracie was sobbing by this point.

I remembered Jenna's counsel to be honest and direct. "No. But I can make you breakfast just like Grandpa does now."

"Great, I always wondered what it would be like to have food poisoning," Ashley said in a voice dripping with sarcasm.

"Hey, I can cook and am perfectly capable of making breakfast."

Ashley raised a brow.

"Okay, so maybe I won't be able to make pancakes quite as good as the ones Grandpa makes, but Kyle can cook. Maybe he will want to make you breakfast."

"It won't be the same," Gracie sobbed.

I pulled her into my lap and gave her a good hard hug. "I'm so sorry I upset you. I guess I didn't handle this as well as I could have. I love Kyle, and I want all of us to be a family. And I know you love Kyle as well. We were happy when we all lived together on Gull Island," I reminded Gracie.

"But Grandpa was there. Doc too." She smashed her face into my shoulder and sobbed.

I glanced at Ashley, who sat quietly with a look of contemplation on her face. I expected that Gracie would be the emotional one, but I expected that Ashley would have raked me over the coals with her sharp tongue by now. Instead, she hadn't said a word since the food poisoning statement. "Ashley," I said. "Do you have any questions?"

She narrowed her gaze. "So since you are our sister, but also sort of like our mother, if you marry Kyle, will he be sort of like our father?"

Okay, where was she going with this? "Yes. I guess so. But you know Kyle. He is really easy going. It's not like he is going to start bossing you around or anything."

Ashley smiled a tiny little smile that barely lifted a corner of one lip. "I know he won't boss me around, but I can ask him about things that I currently ask you about. Right? And his opinion will matter? He won't have to check with you before answering my questions, or making a decision? Like a real father," she emphasized.

I narrowed my gaze. "Yeah. I guess. Did you have something specific in mind?"

Ashley's grin grew bigger. "No. I was just establishing the boundaries of the new relationship we will share with Kyle."

"So you are okay with Kyle and me getting married?"

Ashley shrugged. "I'd like to talk to Kyle first. In private. Then, I'll let you know."

Oh lord, what did that girl have up her sleeve? I turned my attention back to Gracie, who had stopped sobbing but still looked far from happy. "Are you okay?" I asked.

"No."

"Okay, so what has you the most worried?"

"Grandpa." Gracie wiped a hand across her eyes in an attempt to dry them.

"Are you worried he won't be around to make your breakfast and that you will miss his good cooking? If so, we can figure that out."

Gracie shook her head. New tears pooled in the corner of her eyes.

"Okay, so then if you aren't worried about missing out on his good cooking, what is on your mind?"

"Grandpa needs us. He told me that making breakfast for Ashley and me is the main reason he is so happy to get up each morning. Papa has Rosalie, but Grandpa only has us. If we move away, he won't have anyone to make pancakes for. He won't have anyone to be happy for."

I had to hand it to Gracie; she did make a good point. A point I hadn't considered but should have. After my grandma passed away, taking care of me had given Grandpa purpose. He'd told me often that I was the bright spot in the center of his world. I'd eventually grown up and moved away, and I did remember that he'd lost the smile I'd always associated with him once I was gone from his everyday life. But then, the girls came along, and I moved back to the resort, and I guess we gave him a reason to get out of bed each day because his smile had returned. He seemed like a whole new man since they'd come into our lives. And when I'd took off for the east coast while dealing with my own personal issues, he'd packed his bags and followed. Gracie realized what I'd failed to consider, Grandpa needed us even more than we'd needed him.

I pulled Gracie close and hugged her tight. "You're right. I'll talk to Kyle and to Grandpa. We'll figure this out, I promise."

After I tucked the girls in for the night, I called Kyle and filled him in on the situation.

"Don't worry about Ashley, I can handle whatever she has planned, but I am concerned about Gracie. She has such a tender heart. There aren't a lot of kids her age that would pick up on the fact that perhaps a grandfather needed the granddaughter as much as she needed him."

"She is a pretty special kid, and her concern is a real concern. I should have realized how our moving would affect Grandpa."

"I have a huge house, so maybe he can move in here with us," Kyle suggested.

"It would be worth having a discussion with him. He might feel like a third wheel unless we can convince him that we really need him. Maybe we can make a case that we are both so busy that having someone to help out with the cooking and whatnot would be a big help."

"It would be a help, but I also think we need to be honest with him when we speak to him. He will see through any subterfuge, and I don't want him to feel like we are making the request for him to move in with us out of pity."

"Yeah," I agreed. "That would only hurt him. Let's have dinner with the girls tomorrow and see if we can get a feel for where they are after they've had a chance to think things over. They want to go to that new steakhouse."

"I think that is a wonderful choice. Perhaps we should bring them by the house first to talk things through. I'm not sure a public restaurant is the best place to try to talk about something so emotional."

"Okay. I think Ashley has plans with Kristi tomorrow. I'll check with her in the morning and figure out the best time to bring them over. In the meantime, I'll come by early so we can work on digging through the information you find this evening relating to the bombing and rebuilding the town's infrastructure. Have you managed to get into the computer?"

"Not yet, but I'm working on it." Kyle yawned. "To tell you the truth, I am exhausted. I think I'll turn in soon and take another stab at this in the morning."

"Okay. I'll call you after I check with Ashley and Gracie about their plans."

# CHAPTER 13

Sunday, November 12

"I dropped the girls off with Jenna, and plan to pick them up at three," I informed Kyle after arriving at his home the next morning. "We have a dinner reservation at five-thirty, so that will give us time to talk to them about whatever is on their minds. I have no idea what Ashley is up to, and while I know that Gracie adores you, it is very clear that she is having a lot of anxiety about moving into your house full time."

"How do *you* feel about moving into this house full time?" Kyle asked.

I wrinkled my brow. "Honestly. I feel conflicted. I love you so much, and I can't wait to spend my life with you. On the one hand, the idea of sleeping in your arms every night and waking up with you next to me every morning is so incredibly wonderful that I can't believe that it will soon be my reality. On the other hand, except for a few years between high school and the girls coming to live with me, I have lived at the resort for my entire life. Not living there, not waking up to Grandpa's pancakes or Dad's inquiry about my plans for the day is going to seem odd."

"I get that. And I don't want to pressure you into anything. We can have a long engagement or a short engagement or whatever sort of engagement you want. I want you and the girls to be comfortable with the move once you finally make it."

I leaned forward and kissed Kyle on the lips. How on earth had I managed to earn the love of such a totally fantastic guy? He'd loved me through all my moods, all my ups and downs, and all the other relationships I'd had along the way. Of course, I wanted to marry him, and I wanted it to be sooner than later. Now all I had to do was to convince my sisters that living here with Kyle was what they wanted as well.

Once we had settled on our plans for the day, Kyle went into his office to check on the progress of the program he had left running, which he assured me would eventually break the passcode on Harriet's computer, and I went into the kitchen to make a fresh pot of coffee. Once the coffee had brewed, I poured two mugs and took them into Kyle's office. "Any luck?" I asked as I handed one of the mugs to him.

"Actually, yes. I'm in. Now, I just need to find the file where she kept the information relating to the blog. It's not in any of the obvious places. She may even have uploaded the information to the cloud."

"If she did, will you be able to find it?"

"Eventually."

After two hours of trying to be quiet while Kyle worked, I headed over to Jenna's to pick up my sisters. I quickly filled her in on their reaction to the idea of moving to Kyle's and, while Jenna was sympathetic, she did remind me that I needed to be strong and stick to my guns if I didn't want to find myself permanently single. I knew she was right, but when I thought of Grandpa and Gracie's concern for him, my heart broke.

After we left Jenna's, we stopped by the resort so the girls could pick up the dresses they'd wear that night, and then we headed toward Kyle's place. Gracie wanted to bring Pumpkin since Echo was hanging out with Trooper, so I told her that was fine and grabbed his leash and a few toys for the drive. I had to admit I was a lot more nervous about the next few hours than I would have liked. Maybe trying to work out the terms of my engagement to Kyle while we already had so many other things to deal with was crazy. He wasn't going anywhere. Perhaps we should have waited.

Gracie gave Kyle a sincere yet somewhat restrained hug. I wasn't sure if she was being careful of his ribs or if she was protecting her heart. Ashley held up her hand for a high five, and then immediately requested to speak to Kyle in his office. I watched the two of them leave the room with a feeling of dread in the pit of my stomach.

"Do you know what Ashley wants to talk to Kyle about?" I asked Gracie after they were out of sight.

"No. She didn't say. Did you talk to Kyle about Grandpa?"

I nodded. "Kyle and I are going to talk to Grandpa. We know you love him, and we do too. We've discussed a few options, but I really feel I should talk to Grandpa about those options before we discuss the matter."

"Does one of those options include us staying at the resort?" Gracie wondered.

Did it? I supposed that having Kyle move in with us would alleviate Gracie's concerns, but the house was already pretty crowded, and Jenna had been right about the queen bee thing. "No," I finally answered. "I don't think that all of us living in the same house would work. Papa and Rosalie are going to be getting married next month. They are going to want their privacy."

"Are you and Kyle going to want your privacy? Maybe Ashley and I should just move away so we won't bother you."

I hugged Gracie. "You are not a bother to either of us. We love you very much, and if you move away, I'm going with you. We are a team, you, Ashley, and me. Kyle doesn't want to replace anyone; he just wants to join the team. Instead of the three musketeers, we can be the four musketeers."

Gracie crossed her arms over her chest. She was frowning, but I could see by the look on her face that she was thinking things through as well. Gracie loved Kyle, and I really hadn't expected push back from her, but I suppose that the change I was asking of my sisters was a big change and they'd need time to process it.

I managed to talk Gracie into heading out onto the deck so the dogs could play on the snowy beach. When she saw how much fun Pumpkin was having, her mood improved significantly. The two of us decided to make snowballs and throw them for the dogs to chase. Since they tended to break into a million pieces once they hit the ground, the dogs' reaction to chasing a ball, only to have it disappear, was hilarious.

By the time we went back inside, Ashley and Kyle had returned to the living room. Ashley didn't look angry or even sad, but the look of self-satisfaction that she'd arrived with seemed to have been replaced with a look of contemplation.

"So were you able to ask Kyle the questions you wanted to?" I asked Ashley.

"I did."

"So are we good?"

She shrugged. "Maybe."

I looked at Gracie. "Would you like to talk to Kyle alone?"

She looked surprised by my question, but after a moment of hesitation, nodded that she would. I felt my stomach tense once again. Who knew something as simple as getting engaged would be so hard?

"So did your talk go well?" I pried after Ashley and I were alone in the room.

Ashley looked at me, tilted her head, and lifted one shoulder. "It was fine. We are still negotiating, but I think we will be able to come to an agreement."

"Negotiating? About what?"

"It's personal. I'm going to run upstairs and change into my dress. I'm starving, and Kyle said I could order anything I wanted."

*Personal?* Suddenly, I felt totally out of the loop, which was a feeling, I was not fond of in the least.

# CHAPTER 14

Monday, November 13

"You're up early," my dad said when I entered the kitchen a good two hours before I had to get up. Dad had always been an early riser, so I wasn't surprised to find him drinking coffee at the kitchen table.

"I couldn't sleep," I said as I poured myself a cup of the strong dark brew Dad specifically ordered for the resort.

"Can I help?" Dad asked as I sat down across from him.

I wrapped my hands around my coffee and looked across the table. After I moved out, I was really going to miss the early morning conversations we sometimes had. "Perhaps," I answered.

Dad sat quietly, waiting for me to begin.

"Kyle and I are engaged."

Dad expressed shock first and then joy. "Congratulations. Kyle is a great guy. I can't think of anyone I'd rather welcome into the family."

"Thank you. It's pretty new, and we haven't told many people. I want to talk to Grandpa, so I would appreciate it if you didn't mention it until I have a chance to do that."

"Of course. I'm sensing that your inability to sleep is tied into this new development."

I nodded. "I spoke to Ashley and Gracie about it. I knew it would be a difficult conversation, but I didn't know how difficult. They both love Kyle, but neither are really thrilled with the idea of moving, which I totally understand. It was hard on them when Mom died, and now they are settled in here. You have welcomed them and made them feel at home. They feel safe and comfortable. I'm concerned about upsetting the equilibrium we've managed to establish."

"I can understand that. Change, even change you welcome, can be difficult. Has the prospect of moving made the girls angry? Sad? Scared?"

I wrapped my hands around my mug. "Ashley seems to have turned the situation into some sort of negotiation. I don't know everything that happened during her private conversation with Kyle, but I have a feeling that she is negotiating for a raise in her allowance, a later bedtime, or any number of privileges she feels he may grant whereas I have not. I'm not totally sure what she was after, but she specifically asked me if Kyle would be able to make decisions without having to check with me if she were to go to him with a question or problem."

Dad chuckled. "That's our Ashley. Always working an angle."

The corner of my mouth quirked up in a half smile. "Yeah, I really shouldn't be surprised. Ashley does like a good negotiation, but Kyle can handle himself, so I'm not overly worried about her walking all over him, but Gracie... Gracie is really worried about Grandpa."

My dad leaned back in his chair. "I see. What exactly is she worried about?"

"She told me that Grandpa would be sad without us. That it is taking care of us that brings a smile to his face and gives his life meaning. She didn't use those exact words, but that was her concern, and I know she is right."

Dad nodded slowly. "Yes, I would agree with that. After you graduated and left home, he decided his job here was done, and he moved out as well. He told me that he didn't want to be a burden, which was ridiculous since the house that we all lived in is the same house he built with his own hands. When I pointed that out, he told me that he'd passed the resort and the house on to me, and he no longer considered it his home. He moved into that little apartment in town, and to be honest, I was really worried about him. He seemed to be sad and lonely much of the time, but then your mother was killed in the auto accident, and you and the girls moved in with me. It was a really tough time in all our lives, and we really needed Grandpa's help. He knew he was needed, so he called me and told me he was happy to come back and pitch in for as long as we needed him. He's been a different man since the girls have been here. I don't think that Gracie is wrong to worry about how the move will affect him."

That was what I figured. "Kyle and I have talked about asking him to move in with us. You and Rosalie are getting married, and I know you would welcome some privacy. It could be a good solution. I just don't know if he'll go for it."

Dad didn't answer right away. I could see he was thinking things through. I decided to wait for him to work up to saying whatever it was he was going to say. When he finally did speak, I was surprised by what he said.

"I'm happy you found Kyle, and I'm happy you are making plans to build a life with him, and I would never want to do or say anything to dissuade you from that decision. However, if you for one moment think that I'm happy you are moving out, you're wrong. Yes, Rosalie and I are getting married, but that doesn't mean I want to trade the life I plan to build with her, for the life I already have with you and the girls. I know that it is natural for children to one day leave the nest, and I suppose that in a way, I've been preparing myself for that ever since you entered your teen years, but I'm not sure I even have the words to convey how much I will miss you and the girls. I guess I'm greedy and I want it all."

"We aren't leaving town," I pointed out. "You'll still see us all the time."

"I know, but it won't be the same."

He was right. It wouldn't be the same.

"Surely, Rosalie will welcome the opportunity to have the house to herself," I reasoned. "I know she loves you, but I'm not sure she signed up to have a filled to the brim household, and the mess and chaos that comes with a huge extended family."

Dad shook his head. "She never really had a family. She lived alone for a long time, and she has told me on many occasions how happy she is to be part of a big happy family. Having said that, it is natural that you would be excited about having your own home with Kyle. I don't want you to worry about Rosalie and me. We'll be fine."

"And Grandpa?"

Dad furrowed his brow. "I'm not sure. He did follow you to South Carolina, so I suppose that experience might open the door to his being receptive to the idea of living with you and Kyle again. He won't even consider it, however, if he feels like he is a burden. Grandpa needs to feel needed."

I supposed that feeling needed was a byproduct of the human condition. I let out a long breath. "I wish I knew what to do. I want to marry Kyle, and I want to have a life with him, but if I am honest, I have a lot of very mixed feelings about leaving the resort." I reached across the table and put my hands over my father's. "I do worry about Ashley and Gracie and Grandpa. And I do worry about me. Who will I talk to when I can't sleep if I no longer can wander down to this kitchen where I know you'll be waiting?"

"You'll have Kyle. You won't need me."

"I'll always need you. Maybe I'm not ready for this. Maybe Kyle and I are rushing into things."

"Do you really believe that?" Dad asked.

I paused to think about my answer. "No. I love Kyle. I want to marry him, but I don't want to upset the apple cart. The girls are doing so well. Everyone is settled, and they have so much support here at the resort. I think that forcing them to move if they aren't ready would be a mistake."

Dad took a sip of his coffee. "Have you set a date for the wedding?"

I shook my head. "Kyle wants me to be ready. He said he is willing to wait. He wants to be sure that the girls and I all have the time we need."

"Then take it. If you aren't in a hurry, and Kyle is willing to wait, then take the time you need. I have a feeling that if you let things unfold naturally, they'll work themselves out."

"And you are sure that Rosalie isn't secretly wishing she had the place to herself and would welcome us moving out sooner rather than later?"

"I'm sure. If you aren't sure, you should ask her."

I thought about her statement that she wanted to spend as much time with the girls as she could before they grew up and headed off to college. I thought about the sewing room she was planning with Ashley and the smile on her face when she talked about their sewing project. What we had really was pretty perfect, if you eliminated my own pettiness where Rosalie was concerned. I just wished there was a way to keep what we had *and* build a life with Kyle.

# CHAPTER 15

"Two more laps," I yelled at the girls in my second period physical education class. Running outdoors was no longer an option with the fresh snow, so I had the girls running laps around the gym. Once they finished here, we'd head into the weight room, where they would build up their biceps while I tried not to worry myself into a stress coma. I loved my chats with my father, but today, our early morning talk had left me feeling even more confused than I had been before the talk. If I only had myself to consider, it would be so much easier, but I wasn't a solitary tree growing in the middle of an open field. I was part of a complex ecosystem, and as part of that ecosystem, I had the other trees, shrubs, insects, and animals that depended on me to consider. If you really stopped to think about it, every tree in the ecosystem was important. Its presence affected the distribution of sunlight, water, and nutrients in the soil. There really were a lot of variables to consider, and I knew I'd be remiss not to obsess about every one of them.

"Something on your mind?" Principal Remington asked as I pulled myself out of my daydream.

"Trees," I answered. I hadn't heard him approach. How long had he been standing there? How long had my girls been standing around gossiping instead of working out?

"Trees?"

"Really. I was thinking about the effect a single tree can

have on a complex ecosystem. Did you need something?"

"Actually, I did want to speak to you about a phone call I received this morning. Can you come by my office during your prep period?"

I nodded. "Sure. I can do that. Do you need me to bring anything with me? This month's expense report or the schedule for the ski team?"

"No, the business I want to speak to you about is unrelated to school activities." Remington looked toward my class, many of who were sitting on the floor by this point. "Just pop by when you can. For now, I'll leave you to it."

"Okay," I called to the girls. "Your break is over. Let's head to the weight room."

I picked up my clipboard and followed the girls from the gym into the hallway. I really did need to get a grip. I knew that I was doing what I have a tendency to do, which was to make things a lot more complicated than they needed to be. Kyle wasn't pressuring me into setting a date. He wasn't insisting on a timeline for the girls and me to move into his home. I'd opened the door by talking to the girls about the concept of Kyle and me marrying, but perhaps I needed to back off on the immediacy of the whole thing. The way things were now seemed to be working out just fine. During the week, I was home with the girls, but on most weekends, I spent at least one night at Kyle's, giving us some couple time. As long as Dad was right, and Rosalie was fine with all of us living in the house, I didn't see why our current arrangement couldn't continue for the time being.

"Coach Jensen?"

Once again, I was abruptly pulled from my musing to find myself standing in a crowded hallway.

"The door to the weight room is locked."

I actually felt myself blush. "Oh, sure. Sorry, I was thinking about something else." I took the master key to all the rooms in the building that I kept on a string around my neck and unlocked the door. I'd speak to Kyle later and get his take on things. Right now, I really did need to pay attention and do my job.

# CHAPTER 16

"You wanted to see me?" I asked, after poking my head into Greg's office almost two hours later.

"Yes. Thank you for coming by. Have a seat."

I did as instructed.

"I received a call this morning from Kyle. As I'm sure you know, he is working with the remaining town council members to try to get the town back in business."

"Yes. We've talked about it. There are bills to pay, decisions to make, and subcontractors to manage."

Greg steepled his fingers as he worked up to his reason for calling me into his office. "Of course, I'd heard about the bombing and the total destruction of the town hall, but I have to admit that until Kyle and I spoke, I hadn't considered what a huge task was actually at hand. The loss of human life has been at the forefront of everyone's mind, but the loss of the town's files and infrastructure is likely to have an even more far-reaching effect."

I nodded. "It really is a mess. The town is basically closed down at this point. There isn't even a mechanism in place to pay the plow drivers should we have a big storm."

Greg frowned. "Kyle explained that when he called this morning to ask if I would be interested in one of the three town council seats that are open. My first reaction was to be flattered to be asked, which was followed shortly after by a sense of panic at being pulled into what seems, at this point, to be a sinking ship. Don't get me wrong. I have every confidence in Kyle to get things back on track, but I have a feeling that the town council as a whole is looking at some bumpy water before things flatten out."

"The council does have a long and rough road ahead," I agreed, unsure why we were having this conversation. "And I, for one, understand how important it is to find the best candidates the town has to offer to fill the empty seats."

Greg leaned forward, resting his elbows on his desk. "You've worked for me for a number of years now. You've also been close to the town council and its members. Do you think I'd make a good addition to the team?"

Okay, I wasn't expecting that, but I could somehow sense he wanted my honest answer. I took a moment to consider all the names that had been tossed around. I thought about the strengths and weaknesses of each of the names on the list and tried to gauge how each would do with such a difficult task ahead of them.

"Well," I began. "The council is going to need someone who can commit a significant amount of time, at least in the beginning. And this school is a fairly large institution with a lot of moving parts which keeps you pretty busy, so I can see that at times you might encounter conflicts scheduling your time, but you are organized and hardworking, and if anyone can juggle two huge commitments simultaneously, I think you can. As for having the right temperament to be an asset to the community, you are fair and open-minded. You seem to really listen to what people say, and I've known you to consider both sides of a conflict before making up your mind. You are both creative and analytical, so yes, I think that you have a lot to offer. The position won't be easy, but it is important. We need exceptional people to sign on. I'm not certain if you are asking me if you should consider the offer, but if that is what you are asking, then yes, at the very least, I think you should continue your discussion with Kyle and see where it ends up."

Greg nodded. "Thank you. I appreciate your honesty. I will discuss it with my wife. I do understand the urgency of the whole thing, so I assured Kyle that I will make up my mind one way or the other by tomorrow."

I left Greg's office wondering if I had helped Kyle in his campaign to fill the empty seats or if I had hurt it. I supposed in the end, he needed town council candidates who were certain they wanted and were ready for the job, the same way that he deserved a fiancée who was ready and willing to get married and not waffling at every turn.

# CHAPTER 17

Meeting with Greg had put me behind on my paperwork, so by the time I finished up and got everything turned in that needed to be turned in, it was almost time to pick up Gracie from play practice. I was so excited that she was chosen to be part of the annual event, but I would be glad when all the extra running around to take her to practice and pick her up would be over. Thankfully, Kari was in the play as well, so Jenna and I had decided to divide the carpool duties between the two of us.

"I thought I was picking up today," I said to Jenna as I slid into the seat beside her.

"You were, but it was the first day of dress rehearsal, and I wanted to stay and watch. I texted you to let you know I could bring Gracie home if you wanted me to."

I pulled out my phone. She had texted, but I hadn't checked. "I was late getting off today, so didn't check my phone." I looked toward the stage. "The girls sure look cute."

"They really do," Jenna agreed. "I'm going to have to thank your dad for negotiating for Kari to be an Indian Princess instead of a tree. She was so disappointed when the original roles were cast."

"Why do they even have trees? Can't they build trees out of cardboard if they really feel they are necessary? I can't imagine that any kid would actually be happy to be cast as a tree."

"Other than the role of a tree, most of the other parts have lines to memorize. I suppose kids who want to participate but don't want to be responsible for learning lines might welcome the chance to be a tree."

I supposed that much was true.

"How did things go at dinner last night?"

I laced my fingers together and then unlaced them just as quickly. "Dinner was really nice. The girls loved dressing up, and Kyle treated them like princesses. He let them order anything they wanted, including a Shirley Temple that was presented in a fancy glass."

"So they're okay with the wedding plans?"

"I didn't say that. Ashley seems to have turned the whole thing into some sort of negotiation, and Gracie is very upset about leaving Grandpa. She has a point. He does seem to find his meaning in life from his role as caregiver to the girls."

"Yeah," Jenna said in a soft voice. "I can see that. I noticed a real change in his demeanor after they came to live with you and you all moved back out to the resort."

"I spoke to my dad about it. I thought it might make me feel better, but it made me feel worse. I don't think he was trying to make me feel worse, but I could see how bummed he was that the girls and I would be moving out at some point."

"He must have known that would happen," Jenna pointed out.

"Yes, I think he knew, but I also think that he is going to miss the chaos that comes with living in a multigenerational household. I guess I figured that since he and Rosalie were getting married, they'd both be happy for some alone time, but he said that Rosalie loves living in such a big family. He really seems to think she will miss us as well."

Jenna turned to look at me. "You aren't thinking of ending your engagement with Kyle, are you?"

"No," I said with a conviction I really did feel. "I love Kyle. I want to marry him. I want to build a life with him. I just wish I could do that without messing up the ecosystem."

"Ecosystem?"

"I just feel like everything is perfectly balanced as it is." I paused. "Well, except for the two queen bees thing and I think that is my issue and my issue alone. Rosalie does seem to enjoy having the girls around, and Ashley told me that she plans to talk to Dad about turning one of the spare bedrooms into a sewing room for her and Ashley. I know how much you and Kristi enjoy sewing together. I want that for Ashley, but I hate to sew. Rosalie seems to be happy and willing to fill that void and to be honest, I am happy and willing to let her."

"Ashley and Rosalie don't have to live in the same house to sew together," Jenna reminded me. "You will be moving fifteen minutes away. The girls can spend as much time at the resort as they want."

Jenna made a good point. Maybe I really was overthinking things. "Okay, but what about Grandpa?"

"I wish I could say that it is not your responsibility to provide him a purpose in life, but I don't actually feel that way. I think of all the obstacles you have brought up, his place in the lives of the girls is the one to really consider. Have you talked to Kyle about it?"

I nodded. "He suggested that we ask Grandpa to live with us."

"That could be an option. And it would be nice to have an extra set of hands. Have you asked your grandpa about any of this?"

"No. He doesn't even know that Kyle and I are engaged. I just told my dad this morning. I told him not to mention it to anyone until I have a chance to talk to Grandpa. I just wish I knew what I was going to say. I sort of feel like I only have one shot of getting it right."

"I don't think you are giving your grandpa enough credit. He loves you. He isn't going to want there to be a conflict between you."

"Maybe. But I really do want him to consider coming to live with Kyle and me, and I know if I approach it wrong in the beginning, he might decide I am just asking him out of pity and then he'll never go for it."

"Again, I am going to counsel you to simply be honest with him. He is an adult. You can be real with him."

I took Jenna's hand in mine and gave it a squeeze. "Thanks. I think I needed to hear that."

Jenna squeezed my hand back. "That's what best friends are for. To offer advice and moral support."

I glanced back toward the stage where the pilgrims and the Native American's were gathering for a feast. "They really are growing up fast."

"They are," Jenna sighed. "I'm going to miss this when Kari graduates elementary school."

"I know what you mean. The events at the middle school are fine, and I know that Ashley really enjoyed the play she was in earlier this year, but the plays put on by the middle school are so much more polished. They just don't have the heart-tugging appeal of a grade school event." I huffed out a breath. "I guess it won't be all that long before Ashley and Gracie are worrying about how to get on with their own lives without leaving a giant hole in mine."

"The giant hole is a given from the moment you give birth, or in your case, are presented with custody. As a parent, I think it is up to us to find a way to fill that void without making our kids feel guilty for leaving it in the first place."

That, I realized, was going to be easier said than done.

"Look who just walked in," Jenna nudged me.

I turned around to see Margie Holden walk in with Brandy

Baldwin. I waved at the pair, although I had to admit to feeling sort of weird about things now that Sinful Secrets had aired their dirty laundry. The women paused near the doorway leading out to the hallway of the auditorium, spoke to each other for a moment, and then headed in our direction. I imagined they'd talked things over between them and then decided to put on a brave face and approach Jenna and me.

"Margie; Brandy," I greeted.

The women sat down directly behind us. "Tj; Jenna." Brandy said.

"The kids sure look cute," Jenna said, in what sounded to be a casual tone of voice.

"My middle daughter decided not to participate this year, but both my oldest daughter and my youngest are pilgrim girls," Margie informed us.

I wanted to say something about how sorry I was about what had happened to Margie and her middle daughter, but I couldn't think of a single thing to say that wouldn't make things even more awkward than they already were.

"I heard that you were involved in the explosion at the town hall," Brandy said to me.

I nodded. "That's right. I was sitting in the back of the room, so I managed to come out of it with only minor injuries."

"Did you know that it was Harriet behind Sinful Secrets?" Brandy asked. She seemed to be directing her question to both Jenna and me.

"No, of course, not," I answered.

"Harriet had everyone fooled," Jenna seconded.

"She totally destroyed my daughter's life," Margie said. "In fact, Carl and I are planning to move as soon as the holidays are over."

I offered Margie a sincere look of sympathy. "I can't imagine how difficult this must be for your entire family. Harriet was my friend, and I'm sad she is dead, but there really is no excuse for what she did to both of you and the people you care about."

"Did either of you have any idea at all who was behind the hurtful blog?" Jenna asked the women.

Both women agreed that they'd had no idea, although Margie did admit that she had briefly thought it might be Helen since she had shared her deepest secret with her and the next week, everyone in town was being let in on the thing she was the most afraid of and the most ashamed of.

"I'm sorry that you were hurt in the blast, and I'm sorry that Lloyd died as a result of the blast, but I am not sad that Harriet is dead," Margie said. "She got what she deserved."

I really couldn't disagree, given the hurt Harriet had caused for Margie and her family.

"When Roy came by to talk to me about the explosion and told me that Harriet not only appeared to have been the target but that she was also the one behind the blog, I simply couldn't believe it," Brandy said. "I simply couldn't believe that anyone could be so mean. Outing me and the affair I've been having was bad enough, but telling everyone in town about Margie's indiscretion and that Carl was not the father of the daughter he had raised since birth was beyond reproach."

Jenna and I just looked at each other. There really was nothing to say at this point.

"Do you know if Roy ever figured out who killed Harriet?" Margie asked.

"No, not yet," I answered.

"If it was someone the witch outed, then I hope he or she gets away with it," Brandy said.

"Harriet wasn't the only one to die," Jenna pointed out. "Lloyd is dead, Hank is paralyzed from the waist down, and Bookman is only just beginning to heal. I don't disagree that

Harriet may have deserved what she got, but the others who were injured were innocent bystanders. Personally, I hope that Roy does figure out who did this horrible thing for those who died or were injured but really hadn't done anything wrong."

Margie leaned forward slightly. "Brandy and I are outraged by what Harriet did to our families, and we have every right to be, but I do understand innocent people were killed and injured. Roy asked me if I knew of anyone other than myself, of course, who might want to harm Harriet. At the time, I mentioned the other victims of the blog, including the two of you, but he seemed to have all those names. I've been giving it some thought, however, and it occurs to me that perhaps he should speak to Deputy DuPont."

I raised a brow. "Deputy DuPont?"

"I had an appointment at the bank the day before the explosion. As I mentioned before, after the facts relating to my affair were made public, Carl and I decided to move out of the area in order to try for a fresh start, and I wanted to talk to the bank about a loan to help us with moving expenses. As I was walking past the town offices, I saw Deputy DuPont standing just inside the town building. Harriet was standing directly across from him, and it appeared the two were arguing."

"Arguing about what?" I asked. Deputy DuPont worked out of the main county office in Indulgence, and he rarely visited the Serenity office. I'd never known him to visit our small town on the North Shore of Paradise Lake recreationally, so I had to wonder why he was speaking with Harriet.

"I'm not sure," Margie answered. "I could see them yelling at each other, and there was a lot of flailing of arms and sharp gestures, but I saw them through the window, so I wasn't able to hear what was being said."

If Deputy DuPont had been in town the day before the explosion, Roy would have known about it. Wouldn't he? He'd certainly never mentioned it. I supposed I would call him and ask him about it.

A phone call to Roy revealed that Roy had no idea that DuPont had been in Serenity the day before the explosion, or that the man had met and apparently argued with Harriet. He assured me that he would look into the matter, so I decided to leave the task of dealing with the extremely arrogant and unlikable deputy up to him.

# CHAPTER 18

I decided to talk to Grandpa as soon as I got home. Once I did, everyone in the family would know about Kyle and me, and the pressure to pretend nothing was going on would be off. I figured that once everyone was made aware of the situation, the next step would be to allow everyone to get used to the idea of the girls and me moving out at some point in the distant future. I just hoped that could be accomplished without hurt feelings or unnecessary drama.

When I arrived at the resort, Rosalie told me that Grandpa was in the den watching an old western. That was as good a place as any to have our talk, so I headed in that direction.

"Hey, Grandpa. I see you and the Duke have found a way to pass the time on this snowy afternoon." I sat down next to him on the sofa.

"I've seen this movie dozens of times, but it's a good one."

"Since you've seen the movie before, I wondered if it was okay if I talked to you about something."

Grandpa picked up the remote and clicked off the television. "Of course, pumpkin. What's on your mind?"

"I have news to share. Good news, yet still news that has me a bit worried as well."

Grandpa narrowed his gaze. "Okay. Why don't you just tell me what is on your mind, and I'll see if I can help."

I decided to take the direct approach and jumped right in.

"Kyle asked me to marry him. Actually, that's not true. I accepted a proposal that Kyle never actually got around to presenting, but he agreed that was what we wanted, so what I guess I am trying to say, is that Kyle and I are engaged."

Grandpa leaned over and hugged me. "That's wonderful. You know how fond I am of Kyle."

I nodded. "I do. Which is why I hope you will consider this next part."

"Next part?"

"While I am thrilled with the idea of Kyle and me marrying, I am scared of what that will mean for the girls. While Kyle and I don't plan to marry until next summer, or possibly even after that, I am aware that marrying Kyle will mean moving in with him, and I'm afraid that will upset the equilibrium the girls have finally settled into. I've really been stressing about how a move will affect them, which is why I am about to ask you a huge favor."

Grandpa raised a brow. "Favor?"

"Kyle and I talked about it, and we wondered if you would be willing to move to Kyle's place with the girls and me when the time comes? I know you are settled here, but we both feel that you are such an important part of their lives, and having you around to make them breakfast and help look after them really could make all the difference in their ability to adjust. Especially Gracie. You don't have to decide now. Kyle and I aren't getting married right away. Next summer would be the soonest and, like I said, it might not even be then. I love Kyle, but I am not willing to do anything that would destroy the fact that Ashley and Gracie both finally seem settled."

Grandpa didn't answer right away.

"Like I said," I added. "I know what I am asking is a big ask, and you don't have to decide now, but I do hope you will at least think about it."

Grandpa nodded slowly. "Okay, I'll think about it. If you aren't getting married until the summer, then I guess we have time to see how things develop. You know I love you and the girls more than anything, and if you all truly need me, then, of course, I want to be there for you. Having said that, a lot can happen in eight or nine months, which is why I think that waiting to see where we are when the time for the move comes around is the best option at this point."

I hugged Grandpa. "I totally understand. And thank you. You know how much you mean to me and Ashley and Gracie. You bring stability to our lives."

"Have you talked to your dad about this?" Grandpa asked.

I nodded. "I couldn't sleep and got up early this morning. As usual, he was up, so we talked. I told Ashley and Gracie yesterday. I will admit that Gracie didn't take the news well, but Kyle and I talked, and we both agreed that things are fine as they are now for as long as they need to be. We plan to take things slow so that everyone has a chance to get used to the idea of our marrying before we actually set a date."

Grandpa nodded. "I think that is wise, and I admire you and Kyle for putting the needs of your sisters in front of your own needs."

"Honestly," I said, "while I love Kyle and want to marry him, I think I need the time to adjust to the idea too. I don't always do well with change."

Grandpa chuckled. "No, darlin' you really do not."

After I'd spoken to Grandpa, I told Rosalie what was going on, and I had to admit she actually teared up. Of course, she hugged me and told me that she was happy for me, but I could see that the news that the girls and I would be moving out as soon as next summer had affected her deeply. I guess I really had misjudged her. If nothing else, her response made me feel closer to her. I supposed that part of me felt threatened by her presence before, but now that I knew she really did want to have the girls and me around and wasn't just saying that for my dad's benefit, I realized that leaving her might, in the end, be just as hard as leaving everyone and everything else.

After dinner, the girls headed upstairs to work on their homework, and I headed to my bedroom to grade papers and work on my lesson plan. It had started to snow. Not a lot, but the air was filled with flurries. My cat, Cuervo, was curled up on the bed, and Echo was snoring softly from his bed next to mine. I loved evenings like this when I knew that the people I cared most about were here tucked inside the house that my grandpa built all those years ago.

"Can I come in?" Gracie asked from the doorway.

I smiled. "Absolutely." I pulled the comforter that was laid across the bed up so Gracie could snuggle under it. "Why don't you have slippers on?"

Gracie shrugged.

"Is there something on your mind?" I asked as Gracie settled into the pillows I'd stacked up against the headboard.

"The wind is making the tree hit the house near my window. I couldn't get to sleep, so I decided to come into your room. Are you working on school stuff?"

I nodded. "Lesson plans. They aren't my favorite thing to have to do, but Principal Remington likes them to be turned in each month. I watched part of your rehearsal today. You did a very good job."

"Thanks." Gracie snuggled up closer to me. "Did you tell Grandpa about Kyle?" Gracie asked, which I realized was the real reason she had joined me.

"I did."

"Was he sad?"

I paused. "No. I don't think so. Kyle and I aren't getting married until summer at the earliest, so nothing is going to change for a very long time. Grandpa and I both agreed to work together to make everything as easy for everyone as is possible. He has some things to think over, and Kyle and I have some things to think over, but I promise you, that the last thing we want to do is to remove any of the people you love and who love you from your life."

"Maybe Kyle can just move here."

I paused. "That is a suggestion. And one I will definitely talk to Kyle about. We are working on some other options as well." I turned so that I was looking directly at Gracie. "Do you know that I love you?"

Gracie nodded. "Yes, I know."

"And do you know that Kyle loves you?"

She nodded again.

"And do you trust that we would never do anything to hurt you?"

She hesitated but eventually nodded.

"Okay, then. I don't want you to worry about any of this. I want you to trust Kyle and me to figure things out so that everyone is happy."

"Jenna says that sometimes you can't make everyone happy."

"Well, I guess that is true. But Kyle and I aren't going to do anything until we figure everything out. Okay?"

Gracie reached forward and hugged me. "Okay."

# CHAPTER 19

Tuesday, November 14

It snowed two feet overnight, so school was closed, and I was gifted an extra day off. The girls were ecstatic, although I wasn't sure my dad was quite as giddy since he'd let the staff take vacation time until after Thanksgiving when ski season began, which meant he had no one to help him with the snow removal. Once I'd checked in with Grandpa and let him know that there was no school so the girls could sleep in, I grabbed my heavy boots and heavy jacket and headed out into the now sunny day to help out where I could.

"Wow, I can't believe it snowed two feet overnight," I said to Dad, who was gassing up his snow blower. "It was sort of flurrying last night, but it didn't look like things were going to get all that serious."

"Storms blow in that way sometimes," Dad said. "I called the plow service, and they are going to come out and take care of all the roads and driveways. I'll use the big blower to clear the main paths from the house to the road and between the cabins, and if you want to, you can use the small blower to take care of the narrower paths."

It took the two of us the entire morning to clear the main arteries that allowed us to get around the resort. If the resort had been open, we would have had staff on hand to help out with snow removal, but when the resort was closed, it was up to the family to get the job done. Rosalie had headed over to her veterinary clinic, which was housed on the resort property, but well away from the main house. As soon as we were done, Dad headed over there to make sure she didn't need help digging out, and I packed up the dogs and headed to Kyle's house to clear the walkways and decks since I knew that snow shoveling wasn't on his approved activity list. Ashley and Gracie seemed happy watching television with Grandpa, which I supposed did support the idea that he really was needed.

"I'm not going to need to go to the gym for a week," I said to Kyle as I worked on his back deck with the snow shovel he'd provided. He'd called a service to clear the drive and walkways, so I wouldn't need to deal with that.

"I hate that I have to watch you doing all the work. I think the deck is fine for now. Why don't you take a break?"

I was all for that. Not only was I starving, but I was also exhausted. After we'd taken off our wet boots, hats, gloves, and jackets, and stored them in the mudroom, I put on a pot of coffee while Kyle grabbed a couple of pieces of wood and went into the living room to stoke up the fire. I decided to make sandwiches while the coffee was brewing. Settling on grilled cheese, I plugged in the griddle and then buttered slices of bread while I waited for it to heat up. Kyle didn't have any potato chips, which would have been my side of choice, but he did have canned chicken noodle soup, so I opened a can, divided it between two bowls, and put it in the microwave. Once the soup, sandwiches, and coffee were done, I went into the living room to let Kyle know I had lunch, or I guess by this point, an early dinner, on the table.

"What's all of this?" I asked, after noticing that the coffee table, as well as the sofa cushions, were covered with files.

"I worked on Harriet's computer yesterday and dug out all the information I could."

"Did you find anything?"

Kyle nodded. "I'm starving. I'll fill you in while we eat."

I was starving as well, and the food was getting cold, so I agreed. I was surprised Kyle hadn't brought the case up earlier if he'd found something, although I had been pretty busy with the snow removal since the minute I'd climbed out of bed.

"So what did you find?" I asked the minute we had both sat down at the kitchen table.

"First of all, now that we are focusing on Harriet as the intended victim, I decided to call Roy so we could coordinate an effort to look into all the normal things one would look into if any other murder had occurred. He'd already pulled her phone and banking records, and there was nothing that jumped out. We don't have her actual cell phone, work phone, or her work computer since they were destroyed in the explosion, but I did find a copy of her calendar saved to an online account that was linked to her work computer."

"And?"

"And several things. First of all, Harriet had left a reminder on her calendar that she had a lunch date with JM on the day she died."

"Who's JM?"

"I have no idea. Roy didn't either, but he is looking into it."

"I suppose that if she kept her meeting with JM, then this person could be the one to give her the bomb."

"Roy and I thought so as well. He is taking the lead very seriously. He also spent a good amount of time on Sunday canvassing Harriet's neighborhood and talking to her neighbors. He hoped to find someone who had noticed something."

"Something like what?"

"A new person in her life. Unusual patterns in behavior or

perhaps unusual travel patterns. Anything at all that would provide information as to what was going on in her life prior to the explosion."

I took a bite of my sandwich. "And did he find anything?"

"Not really. At least not as of yesterday, which was the last time I spoke to him, but I could tell that he has no intention of giving up until he figures this out."

I frowned and sat back in my chair. "So what has Kate been doing all this time? I haven't heard her name mentioned since the beginning."

Kyle looked surprised at my question. "I'm sorry. I thought I told you. Kate took an emergency leave from work. I don't have all the details, but apparently, she had a family emergency and left town on Saturday morning. Roy isn't sure when she will be back."

I was sorry to hear that Kate had a family emergency, but not all the bummed to find out that I didn't have to worry about tripping over her as we continued with our investigation. Of course, now Roy was on his own again, which was not going to make things any easier on him. I supposed that Kyle and I would have to pick up the slack and pitch in even more than we had been. Of course, I had sisters to parent and a job to do, so I couldn't commit all my time to the investigation, and Kyle had a town council to put back together, so his time was limited as well.

"Okay, so between you and Roy, you managed to establish that there was nothing odd in her phone or banking records and that she was scheduled to have lunch with JM on the day she died. Do we know where they had lunch?"

Kyle shook his head. "The note just said 'lunch JM' on that date. The time and location were not noted, but as I said, Roy is looking into it."

"Okay, so what else?"

"I'm close to getting into an online storage account I found a link to amongst Harriet's things. I'm hoping the account contains her blogs and the notes for her blog. I haven't forgotten that her home office was trashed leaving me to believe that someone thought she had something they didn't want to be revealed."

"How long will it take you to complete the hack?" I asked.

"I'm hoping to be in by the end of the day; tomorrow morning at the latest. If we don't find an obvious reason for someone to have killed Harriet in the file, I'm afraid we'll be back to square one. Roy has been working long hours, but so far, none of his leads have panned out."

I did feel sorry for Roy. This was not an easy case. "I noticed you had a bunch of files on the coffee table."

"They are all the files I took from Harriet's home office. Given the fact that her office was tossed, I have a feeling the file with the actual motive for her murder, if there even was a file, is long gone, but I decided to wouldn't hurt to take a look at what else she was up to. Roy had one of his temps gather up all the files and loose paperwork that he'd found in her home and bring them to me. There is a lot. Most of it is probably totally irrelevant to whatever is going on, but it needs to be looked through and eliminated just in case."

I had to smile. "You're a good guy, Kyle. It sounds like the town should put you on the payroll."

Kyle chuckled. "You aren't wrong; however, I don't need the money so I'll just consider this my civic duty."

I got up, grabbed the coffee pot, and refreshed both our mugs. "I spoke to Greg yesterday. He told me that you offered him one of the open council seats."

Kyle nodded. "Jeff and I spoke to Bookman. We decided to start by offering the open seats to Greg, Rita, and Doc. I did talk to your dad, but as you suspected, he wasn't interested. To be honest, I pretty much expected Greg, Rita, and Doc to turn down the offer as well, but Rita accepted right off the bat, and Greg and Doc said they'd think about it."

"So what made you decide to ask Rita instead of Brandon?"

"You made a very good point when you suggested her. She is just as qualified as Brandon is, and it would be nice to have at least one female town council member. I was happy she accepted, and hope the other two will as well. I know Greg is busy, so it might not work for him, although he does have a certain amount of flexibility in his schedule. Still, Bookman said he'd worked with him on a grant for the high school arts program, and it was his impression that the man was not only very intelligent but organized and proactive as well."

"I agree. Greg is a great guy and would make a wonderful addition to the council. Not only is he intelligent and hardworking, but I've known him to be fair and open-minded as well. It's rare for the entire staff of a high school to be a fan of the principal, but in Greg's case, I can't think of a single staff member who doesn't admire and truly like him."

"I'm convinced. He needed to speak to his wife about it, which is fair because the council will take up some of his nights and weekends. He said he'd get back to me today, but with the snow, it might be tomorrow. Doc was a bit less certain and wanted to noodle on it a bit, but he said he'd get back to me by the end of the week. He has the time, and he has a unique skill set that will come in handy. My sense was that he wasn't sure he wanted to make that sort of a commitment, but I also think he feels bad that Bookman, Jeff, and I are left to deal with this total mess and he wants to help out if he can."

I bobbed my head. "I bet he does it. Even if he only agrees to a limited term, he is the sort to roll up his sleeves and pitch in when there is something that needs to be done."

"I hope so. I think he could really help."

Kyle got up and began clearing the plates, and I pitched in to help. Poor Kyle. He looked exhausted. Between trying to put the town council back together, taking care of town business, and helping to figure out who blew up the town hall, the guy had a lot on his plate. And if you threw Thanksgiving on top of all of that, I was afraid it was too much.

"Maybe we should consider moving Thanksgiving back to the resort. It is a lot of work to host such a huge gathering, and you already have so much to deal with."

Kyle shook his head. "No. I want to do it. I spoke to Rosalie, and between her and Ben, they have assured me that they will take care of the hams, turkeys, and rolls. Jenna and Frannie are bringing desserts, and my mom is going to tackle the vegetables. We just have to make mashed and sweet potatoes and a few appetizers. I figure that between you and me, Ashley and Gracie, your dad and Rosalie, my mom, Kiara, and Annabeth, your grandpa and Doc, Jenna and her family, Bookman and Helen, Frannie and Hazel, that is only nineteen people. Quite a few less than normally attend. Is there anyone I am missing?"

"I think that is the main gang, although we should ask Bree, Pastor Dan, and Hannah, which will bring us to twenty-two." I felt a pull at my heart. "I can't believe so many people who attended last year's Thanksgiving feast are no longer with us."

Kyle took my hand in his. He gave it a squeeze. "It has been a tough year." He kissed my forehead. "But this year will be better. Things are really up in the air right now, but once we get everything back on track, things will be better."

It felt to me that Kyle was trying to convince himself of this fact even more than he was trying to convince me.

"Maybe we should hold off on making the big engagement announcement for a while. I'm not sure that Thanksgiving is the best time to do it."

Kyle frowned. "Are you having second thoughts about the

engagement?"

"No. Not at all," I assured Kyle. "But the girls need time to adjust to the idea, and I just feel like our announcement would be tainted by the fact that Harriet is sure to be on everyone's mind this Thanksgiving. I want our announcement to be a happy occasion associated with only happy thoughts. I've told everyone in my immediate family, and I know you told your mom. In a way, telling folks as we see them, rather than making a huge announcement, seems like it might be the better way to go. Although..."

"Although what?" Kyle asked.

"Although once we make it public, people will start asking about a date. I told the girls we'd wait to settle on a date until everyone has had a chance to get used to the idea and we'd had a chance to work through their issues, especially Gracie's."

Kyle kissed me gently on the lips. "I agree with everything you have said. And I'm fine with waiting to make an announcement. I really do want Ashley and Gracie to know that their feelings matter and I want you to take the time you need as well."

I put my hands on Kyle's cheeks. "And that is just one of the many reasons I love you so very much."

# CHAPTER 20

Wednesday, November 15

Kyle called me the next morning to let me know that he had gotten into Harriet's personal online storage system. He asked if I had the day off as I had the previous day, but as of this morning, school was back on. I did have a number of vacation days saved up, however, and this did seem important, so I called Greg and explained the situation, and he offered to get me a sub. I dropped the girls off at school and then headed over to Kyle's.

"It was nice of Greg to give you the day off."

"He wants us to figure this out as much as anyone, and I do have a bunch of vacation days saved up. What did you find in Harriet's saved documents?"

"The notes for the November blog for one thing. As far as I can tell, the blog has not been written yet, but if Harriet had actually used the notes in the file, I suspect there would have been a lot of people standing in line to wring her neck."

I cringed. "Okay. Part of me doesn't even want to know what she had dug up if her plans for the November blog were that bad. Still, given the fact that her home office was ransacked, it does look as if at least one of the individuals who would have been targeted in an upcoming blog might actually make a better suspect than the individuals affected by a past blog. What was she planning to write?"

"Unlike past blogs, she had notes on four individuals rather than three in a file marked November blog. Victim number one is Jennifer Black. She owns the bakery that recently opened on the north side of town."

"I know who she is, although I've never actually spoken to her. I don't think she has lived in the area very long. What did she do, or I guess I should say, allegedly do?"

"She allegedly buys her baked goods at a bakeshop in Carson City, and then resells them in Serenity claiming that they are her family recipes."

I raised a brow. "I suppose she wouldn't want that getting out. I can see that it might destroy the business she is just getting started. I wonder how Harriet even found out about something like that."

"I don't know. And I don't know if it is true. But it does seem that if Harriet had revealed that Jennifer is reselling someone else's baked goods and marketing them as her own, it would have hurt her business whether it was true or not. Still," Kyle paused, "I'm not sure that exposing Jennifer's false advertising would warrant her blowing up an entire building."

I sort of doubted Jennifer was the potential bomber we were looking for. "Who else do we have?"

"Girard Bowman. Apparently, he has been stepping out on his wife."

Girard Bowman was a man's man. He was tall, built, and an ex-football player who had a reputation with ladies. He liked to hunt and fish, and he owned his own taxidermy shop. I supposed in terms of having a violent nature, he might fit the profile of a man who would kill someone, although, in terms of motive, he seemed more like the sort to brag about an affair rather than to kill over it. "Who is he allegedly sleeping with?"

"Will Colter."

"Will Colter. The guy who owns the dance studio?"

Kyle nodded.

"I didn't realize Girard was gay. I mean, he is married. To a woman," I emphasized.

"He is, and I hadn't a clue he was gay either. Keep in mind he might not be, but if he is and Harriet was about to out him, I could definitely see him wanting to stop her."

"Well, yeah. He has to be our killer. I can totally see him blowing up a room full of people just to watch the fireworks. The guy is a real scary sort."

"I agree that he seems capable of something like setting off a bomb, but I do think we should follow up with victim number four as well."

"Victim four? What happened to three?"

"Victim number three was going to be Lloyd Benson. Not only is it impossible to follow up with him, but I doubt he blew himself up."

"Lloyd? What did Harriet have on Lloyd?"

"According to the notes, which keep in mind are nothing more than unverified rumors at this point, Lloyd bribed Mayor Wallaby to push through several of his developments back when Wallaby was mayor. According to the notes I found, Harriet was going to use that information to make the case that he should be kicked off the town council and that any and all future developments he might sponsor within the town limits should be denied."

"Wow."

"Wow is right. If that is true and Sinful Secrets would have revealed it, then it could have made things very difficult for Lloyd. Especially if the rumor turned out to be true and Harriet had proof of the dirty dealings."

"If Lloyd hadn't been a victim of the bomber, I would totally have suspected him. But I agree, it is unlikely he blew himself up, and it does look as if he might have been behind the emergency meeting, so who is victim number four?"

"Victim number four is Kate Baldwin."

"Kate Baldwin? Officer Kate Baldwin? Roy's new partner and my new pain in the backside? That Kate Baldwin?"

Kyle nodded. "Apparently, when Kate was in college, she was arrested for attacking a woman named Jackie Leman, who she accused of being responsible for her father's death."

I narrowed my gaze. "If I remember correctly, Kate's father was a cop who died in the line of duty when she was a kid. I don't remember if Kate ever said how he died, I assumed he was shot. Did this woman shoot him?"

"No. I called and spoke to Roy, and he said he'd look into it. He called me back a while ago to let me know that Jackie Leman was the daughter of the murder victim whose death Kate's dad was investigating at the time of his death."

"On the first night we met Kate, she told us that her dad died in the line of duty, trying to protect civilians who shouldn't have been anywhere near a crime scene in the first place. I wonder if Jackie was one of the civilians she was talking about."

"Perhaps. That might explain why she attacked the woman. Harriet's notes didn't go into detail as to why Kate attacked the woman, only that she had and that she was arrested for assault and battery."

I frowned. "So Kate killed Harriet because she was going to reveal that she had a record? I guess that her tainted past isn't something she would want to get around, but to kill someone to keep it quiet. It seems like a stretch."

"I agree. But in my book, it does make Kate a suspect, especially when you add in the fact that she left town for a vague family emergency just as the investigation into the bombing got started."

"That's a good point. Was there anything else in the file?"

"There was a file with additional security attached to it. I'm working on getting into it, but the security is pretty sophisticated."

"Seems odd that Harriet would have a file with that level of security."

"I agree. I don't know who set up the security for the file, but I'm sure it wasn't Harriet. Anyway, it may take a while, but I'll get in. In the meantime, I found a list of passcodes, one of which will allow me to access the town's files."

"Didn't you already have access to the town's files?"

Kyle shook his head. "No, the only people with access were Bookman, as mayor, and Harriet. I asked Bookman for the passcode, which he gave me, but Harriet had changed it. In fact, it looks as if she changed the town's passcode the day before she died. Bookman didn't remember receiving a new code. Maybe Harriet gave it to him, and he forgot, or maybe she never gave it to him. There is no way to tell at this point. Anyway, once I finally got into Harriet's system, and realized she had a master password sheet, which included the password for the town's online file storage, I was able to use that code to get into the town's files."

"Did you find anything interesting?"

"Not really, although I have really only touched the surface in terms of examining the files. It is going to take some time. In the meantime, I thought we might see a woman about a donut, and after that, we might want to check into either getting something stuffed or dance lessons for the girls."

I raised a brow. "So we follow up with the easier leads. Works for me, although the girls already take dance lessons from Miss Marsha."

"We don't need to sign them up. I just figured it would be an ice breaker."

"We should go now. I need to pick my sisters up from school at three."

# CHAPTER 21

Sweet Perfection was a cute shop I supposed if you were into pink and green. I was pretty sure that Ashley would adore the décor, but personally, it wasn't my taste. Still, the aroma of cookies baking when you walked in the front door could not be denied. If Jennifer was buying her baked goods in the valley and then reselling them, she was smart enough to have something in the oven to provide a wonderful aroma for atmosphere.

"Can I help you?" A short woman with short blond hair standing behind the counter asked.

"Everything looks wonderful," I honestly said, as I inventoried the selection displayed in the glass case. "I understand that your baked goods are made from family recipes."

The woman nodded. "My grandmother was a wonderful baker. When she passed away, she left my sister, Lacy, and I each a file box full of family recipes. The recipes were so delicious and so unique that we decided to open a bakery."

"So Lacy works here with you?"

The woman shook her head. "No. Lacy works at the first Sweet Perfection Bakery in Carson City. We opened it together a year ago and did so well that we decided to branch out and add a second store here in Serenity."

I glanced at Kyle. It sounded like Jennifer had been buying the pastries she resold from her own bakery. "I guess having two kitchens must allow you to offer more of a selection."

Jennifer nodded. "The bakery in the valley is much larger. I live in the valley, so I make a lot of what I sell in this store in the kitchen down there. At least for now. Lacy has help running the counter, but so far, it is just me at this location, which makes baking and running the front at the same time pretty tricky. The pastries are all fresh, however. If you can't decide, I have a sampler tray."

"That would be great. We'll take a sampler and two coffees."

So much for Harriet's juicy piece of gossip. It wasn't even true. Well, I supposed technically, it was true, but given the situation, it was far from shocking, and the pastries were to die for. In all fairness to Harriet, Kyle had only found notes pertaining to the bakery. There was a chance that Harriet would have looked into things further and not printed the piece about the bakery had she lived.

"So I wonder if the rumor about Girard and Will is equally yawn-worthy," I wondered after we had left the bakery with a takeout box filled with donuts.

"I don't know. Maybe. But to be honest, I sort of doubt it. I'm not even sure how to handle the interview. Do we simply come out and ask Girard if it is true and if he blew Harriet up because of it?"

I frowned. "No, I don't think that would be the way to approach it. Girard owns that taxidermy shop next to Guns and Roses. I guess we'll just stop by and talk to him. Maybe he will volunteer something or create an opening for us to bring it up."

Kyle frowned. "Seems unlikely, but I'm game to try. I'm not sure we want to do or say anything to get on the guy's bad side."

"I totally agree. The guy is about as scary as they get. In fact, every boogeyman I ever imagined when I was a kid looked pretty much like him."

"The guy does seem formidable."

After we pulled up out in the front, I began having second thoughts. "Maybe we should let Roy handle it. He does have a gun, and we don't."

"Do you really think he is dangerous?" Kyle asked.

"We do suspect him of blowing up a building with seven people inside. Yes, I think that in the right circumstance, he could be dangerous."

Kyle looked at the building. "I guess we could talk to Will first. Get a feel for things."

"Yes," I said, "let's do that."

Of course, it was at that moment that the man walked out and approached the car. The windows were up, so he knocked. Kyle lowered the passenger side window halfway, which had me scooting toward the middle of the seat.

"I noticed you sitting out here, staring at my shop. Can I help you with something?" Girard asked.

"We were debating whether a taxidermist works with family pets that have passed on and not just hunting trophies," I blurted out the first thing I could think of which was incredibly gross and made me want to puke.

"You want to stuff your little fluffy friend?"

"Well, not really," I admitted. "We just noticed the shop which a friend of ours mentioned and the subject came up. For future reference only," I added quickly, "we don't actually require the services of a taxidermist at this point."

"And who friend might that be?" Girard asked.

"Will. Will Colter."

The man smiled, showing off smokers' teeth that were more brown than white. "You know Will?"

"Not well," I answered. "But well enough to have overheard him mention this place. Another friend, Harriet Kramer, mentioned it as well."

I watched as the man's smile faded into a scowl. "If you are friends with that liar, you are not a friend of mine. Now get along. Both of you. And don't darken my door again."

Kyle pulled away from the curb. "Well, the man certainly doesn't like Harriet."

"The fact that he called her a liar seems to indicate that he might know her secret identity."

"Or they could have come to heads over something else," Kyle pointed out. "He does own a business, and Harriet had been in charge of such tasks as collecting business license fees. Maybe she claimed not to have received his payment when he knew he had paid, so he figured she was lying. We don't know enough to come to any hard conclusions, but I do agree that the man should be interviewed by someone with a gun. We'll talk to Roy about him when he checks in with us later."

I scooted back to the passenger side of the vehicle and clipped on my seatbelt. "Since we seem to have hit a dead end, how about we hit up a couple of the lunch places where Harriet may have met JM on the day she died. Maybe someone saw her and can tell us who JM is."

Kyle started the engine. "Roy was going to look into it, but if he hasn't had the chance yet, I'm game. I'll call him and ask him what he has been able to find out so far."

A call to Roy confirmed that he had checked four restaurants near the town offices and hoped to check The Antiquery today, but he'd been held up with another case. Kyle assured him that the two of us wanted to grab a sandwich and that we'd ask the staff about Harriet and her lunch with JM while we were there.

"It feels odd to be heading to The Antiquery. I haven't eaten there since Jenna and Helen sold the place, but I hear the food is still good, so maybe we'll grab a bite while we are there. We did just eat all those pastries, so maybe something small, like a sandwich."

"We could even order something to go. It would give us a chance to chat with the hostess while we wait for our order."

"That's a good idea."

While the establishment looked much the same as it had before Jenna decided to sell it two months ago, knowing that I wouldn't find Jenna in the kitchen made the experience feel a bit different. Jenna had sold to a group of her own employees, which meant that very little had changed on the surface, and most casual customers might not even realize that the restaurant was under different ownership.

"Kyle; Tj. How are you both?" The hostess, a fortyish woman named Natalie who had worked at The Antiquery for about three years and was part of the group that bought Jenna out, greeted.

"We're good. We are actually here for two reasons. The first reason is to grab a sandwich to go, and the other is to ask the employees if anyone remembers Harriet having lunch here on the day the town hall blew up."

"She was here. She sat in a booth in the back with a woman I'd never seen before."

A woman. That was interesting. For some reason, I was expecting a man. "What did the woman look like?"

"Short. No more than five feet tall. She was thin, yet fit looking. She had long black hair. Down to her waist, yet it was sort of raggedy and untrimmed. If I had to guess, she grew it out for convenience and not to make a fashion statement."

"Do you remember her eye color? What she wore?"

"Dark eyes. Brown. She wore jeans and heavy boots. She had on a black t-shirt, and she wore something on a gold chain around her neck. I guess it was a necklace of some sort. I didn't get a good look at it because after she came in, she tucked it under her t-shirt, but it wasn't a dainty diamond. It was bulky."

"Like a medallion of some sort?"

"Not really. It wasn't solid like a medallion. It's hard to describe."

"Could you draw it?" I asked.

Natalie shrugged. "I'm not much of an artist, and I didn't get a good look at it, but I can try."

"Did you notice any other distinguishing features? A tattoo? Scar? That sort of thing."

"I did notice that this woman had a long thin scar over her right eye. The scar wasn't really distracting since it ran along the brow line, but it was noticeable."

"Do you know what Harriet and this woman talked about?" I asked.

Natalie shook her head. "They were quiet, and they stopped talking whenever anyone approached."

"Did you notice if the woman carried a package?"

Natalie furrowed her brow. "No. I don't remember a package. Or even a purse. Harriet was already here when she arrived. The woman walked in, approached the hostess desk, and asked for Harriet. I waved Ginger over, and she took her to Harriet's table. I don't remember that the woman was carrying anything. I'm pretty sure her hands, arms, and back were empty, so no package, purse, or backpack."

"Is Ginger working today?" I asked.

"Yeah. Hang on, and I'll get her. She is working in the back room."

Kyle and I asked Ginger all the same questions we asked Natalie, and she answered with the same responses. She also agreed that the woman didn't have anything in her hands when she arrived. We confirmed that Harriet paid for the lunch with a credit card and that both women left at the same time, but in different vehicles.

"Okay, what should we do now?" I asked.

"I guess we will head back to my place, eat our sandwich,

and wait to hear from Roy. Hopefully, he will be able to talk to Kate, and we can eliminate her from the suspect list."

Shortly after we returned to Kyle's, Roy called and asked to come by. Once he arrived, he shared that he'd spoken to Kate and that their conversation had left him feeling even more uncertain than before he'd called her.

"So what's going on?" I asked, after Kyle, Roy, and I were gathered around Kyle's dining table with fresh cups of coffee.

"As we discussed, I called Kate and told her about the notes Harriet had in her file. I guess I was expecting denial, but instead, she told me that her life before coming to Paradise Lake was none of my business, and it would serve me well to remember that. She was short and impatient during the entire conversation, and after only a brief exchange, she told me that she was needed and had to hang up. And then she did. Just like that. No offer to chat later or to check in. No offer of a timeline for her return to work. Nothing. I could sense that she was stressed."

"Her behavior does make her seem guilty," I said. "Still, I can't see her blowing up an entire building to keep the fact that she had been arrested in the past from coming out. It's not like she killed anyone. Assault is a serious charge, but not that serious."

Roy shook his head. "I don't know what was behind her behavior, and I agree that she seems guilty based on her response. Maybe there is more going on than we've managed to figure out so far. I don't want to think she would hurt anyone unless a show of force was absolutely required, and maybe that is naïve, but I agree with you, I can't see that she had a good enough motive to blow up an entire building. Something feels wrong. If Harriet was the intended victim as we now suspect, why wouldn't the person who wanted her out of the way simply shoot her? Or stab her? Or do anything other than setting off a huge explosion."

"Those are the exact same questions I have asked myself over the course of the past two weeks. I know we have dug into this from a number of different angles, but I still feel like we are missing something."

Roy nodded. "I agree. There has to be more to this. Kate wouldn't do such a thing."

"That is the same thing we both thought about Tim." I reminded Roy about his previous partner, who had turned out to have done exactly what it had looked like he'd done.

"I do remember what happened with Tim, and I do think we need to move Kate to the top of our suspect list, but I also agree that something feels off about this whole thing," Kyle said. "There is that one secure file that I found amongst Harriet's files, and there are the anomalies I noticed in the town's records. Maybe getting to the bottom of both will help us figure things out. I'll work on it and see what I can come up with."

Roy nodded and thanked us both. I felt so bad for the guy. He not only looked exhausted but totally defeated as well. I wasn't a huge fan of Kate Baldwin, but for Roy's sake, I really did hope she'd turn out to be innocent.

# CHAPTER 22

Friday, November 17

I hadn't seen Kyle since Wednesday, but we'd spoken on the phone, so I knew that both Doc and Greg had agreed to give the town council a shot. Kyle had put an ad in the paper for a new town clerk/mayor's secretary and had over twenty applicants reply, most of whom on paper seemed to be fairly qualified. The new town council was set to meet at Bookman's house next week to go over the applications and make a decision.

After a ton of man hours tracking down those affected by the blog, it didn't look as if a single person really stood out as a strong suspect other than Kate, who still wasn't talking. Add to that the fact that the bomb was said to have cost the person who purchased it a pretty penny, and it really narrowed down the suspect pool to, well, to no one. Besides the cost, the whole thing made no sense. If Harriet was targeted by an individual she hurt in her blog, why on earth would they buy an expensive bomb and plant it in her purse? Why wouldn't the killer, as we'd all asked multiple times, shoot her, stab her, or even poison her? Killing her in such a very expensive and unmanageable fashion made no sense, no matter how you looked at it.

There had to be something important that we were missing.

Something that made the *how* make as much sense as the why. We knew that finding the person who did this terrible thing was not going to be easy, so Kyle and I both decided that while we needed to continue to look for answers, we needed to live our lives as well.

"Okay, listen up," I said in a loud voice to get the attention of my sixth period class. "As I'm sure you are aware, we are off for fall break next week. All after school sports practices will be canceled as well, so relax and have a wonderful Thanksgiving."

Ah freedom, I thought to myself as the girls from my last class filed out into the hallway. An entire week to sleep in, spend time with Kyle, and of course, dig into the investigation that seemed to have everyone stumped. Not that I was necessarily going to have any more luck than Roy and Kyle had had during the course of the week, but at times a fresh pair of eyes and a new perspective could make all the difference.

I picked up the few items I planned to bring home just in case I decided to work on my lesson plans, which I highly doubted. I loved my job, but with everything else that was going on, I really was pretty excited to switch gears for an entire week.

"Ms. Jensen, you have a call on line one," The secretary from the front office said over the intercom.

"Thank you." I picked up the line. "Coach Jensen," I answered.

"Tj, it's Gina."

"Gina? Oh my god, how is everything? Do you love your new job? Your new home? How is your hottie boyfriend?" Gina Roberts was a total genius who used to teach math at the high school, but after being kidnapped this past summer and reconnecting with an old flame who lived on the east coast, she'd decided to quit her job at Serenity High and take another chance on love.

"The job is great, and Jeremy and I are doing fantastic. I

really do want to catch up with you about all that, but I'm calling for another reason."

I frowned. "Oh. What's on your mind?"

"I heard about what happened. With Harriet and the town hall."

"Yeah," I said. "It was pretty awful. We still haven't found out who is behind the whole thing."

"Which is why I am calling. I understand that Kyle has been working on gaining access to the town's files."

"He has, and he was having no luck hacking in, but then he managed to hack into Harriet's personal files, and she had a list of passcodes which he used to get into the town's files. Why are you asking? Did you hear about Sinful Secrets?"

"Sinful Secrets?"

"Never mind. Go on. You were asking about the files?"

"Yes, well," Gina paused. She took a moment and then continued. "Is there another landline you can use to call me back? One that isn't part of a larger system?"

"I can call you back when I get home," I offered. "Or if this is really top secret, Kyle has a secure line."

"Actually, I'd like to speak to Kyle as well. If you don't mind calling me back from his secure line, I'll give you a number to call."

"Okay. Hang on." I opened my desk drawer and took out a piece of paper and a pen. "Okay, go ahead."

Gina gave me the number. "When you call, you will hear a double click. Don't hang up. That will just mean that your call is being rerouted."

I frowned. What on earth was going on with Gina? Yes, she did work for a company that dealt with supersecret tech stuff, but the level of security she seemed to be after, combined with her questions about Harriet had me completely stumped.

I called my dad and told him what was going on. He agreed

to pick the girls up from school and to help Gracie get ready for the play if I didn't get home in time. Once that was arranged, I called Kyle, gave him a brief overview, and let him know I was on my way over. As it turned out, the conversation we were about to have with Gina was even more absurd than any of the scenarios my imagination had come up with during my drive to Kyle's place.

"Thanks for going to all the trouble to have a secure discussion with me," Gina started off.

"No problem. What's going on?"

"I have something to tell you, but you have to promise not to get mad."

God, I hated discussions that began like that since the chances were that mad was exactly what I was going to be. "Okay. I promise. What's up?"

Gina took a deep breath and let it out. "Okay, so you remember last summer when I was working for Bristow, and we were trying to get approval for his development."

"Yeah. So? We both know that I was a bit ticked off that you were working for that snake, but I got over it. What does that have to do with this?"

"Well, you see," Gina hemmed and hawed. "We sort of needed some information that was unavailable to us that we felt could nudge a few of the holdouts on the committee onto our side. Since the information was not public record, we couldn't just request it, so I sort of hacked into the town's records."

"You hacked into the town's records to help Bristow?" I was almost speechless. I'd hated Bristow for trying to blackmail Mayor Harper before he died, and I really couldn't understand why Gina would have agreed to work for him even if she did need the money, but to break the law for him. Sure, Kyle hacked into stuff all the time, but that was different. He was one of the good guys, and he used his superpower to make the world a better place. "So what does this have to do with Harriet?" I eventually asked.

"Well, you see when I hacked into the town's system, I realized that I might very well need to get back into the town's records at some point in the future, so I created a back door. I figured it would cut down on the amount of time needed to hack back in."

"You created a back door to the town's files?"

"I did," Gina admitted. "Actually, I have backdoors into lots of places, but I guess that isn't the point. The point is that I don't necessarily want other hackers to use my back door, which if found, they certainly could do, so I set up alarms."

"And I set off the alarm when I tried hacking in," Kyle said.

"Yes, you did. I figured it was you, and I wasn't overly concerned. I'd even planned to tell you how to get in, but then you managed to get in yourself. Tj told me that you found the passcode in Harriet's personal files. Anyway, I realized that I really should close the back door I had created and get out of the system altogether, so I went in to remove the alarms and found that someone else had hacked into the town's files since I'd last been there."

"Someone else?" Kyle asked. "Who?"

"I don't know who tried to hack in specifically, but I do know that the person who tried to hack in, did so from a computer housed within the South Shore office of the Paradise County Sheriff."

"DuPont," I breathed.

# CHAPTER 23

"I cannot believe how adorable Gracie and Kari look," I whispered to Jenna that evening while we watched the school play. Both the Jensen and Elston families had turned out for the event, so it was a group of twenty who all sat together.

"The little boy who is playing the turkey is so funny," Grandpa, who was sitting behind me, leaned forward and whispered in my ear. "He keeps tripping over those much too big feet, but he seems to be rolling with it just fine."

"I think he might be tripping on purpose for comic effect," Dennis, who was sitting on Jenna's other side whispered. "No one can be that clumsy naturally."

"Oh, I don't know," Doc, who was sitting in the row behind me, countered. "The look on his face as he starts to fall seems to be unrehearsed to me."

"We are almost to Gracie's lines," Kyle shushed us.

"I hope she doesn't blow it," Ashley mumbled.

I held my breath as Gracie said the lines that she had been rehearsing for days. I only let it out when the lines were delivered flawlessly.

"That's our girl," I heard my dad say.

"She really is very good at speaking clearly so as to be understood," Rosalie added.

I glanced at the group gathered around me and smiled. It felt good to be in the center of a large family who cared about each other and the everyday moments of their lives. I was sad that my mom had died early in life, but I was also happy that Ashley and Gracie had been given the opportunity to grow up in a nurturing environment.

"Doc and I are going for pie," Grandpa said to Bookman and Helen after the play was over. "Would the two of you like to join us?"

"Actually, I think we'll just head home," Bookman said. "I'm getting a little tired."

"Tj? Kyle?" Grandpa asked.

"The girls are going to the home of one of their classmates for a sleepover. I think that Kyle and I are going to head over to his place. Just so you do not worry, we have Echo."

"Rosalie and I will go with you," my dad responded to Grandpa's query.

"Jenna? Dennis?"

"Date night." Jenna hugged her handsome husband's arm.

"And I have a sermon to prepare," Pastor Dan said, as he smiled at Bree, who was holding onto his daughter, Hannah's, hand. "I will see you all on Sunday."

"It was nice that everyone came out for the play," Kyle said as we walked hand in hand toward the parking lot.

"Yes. We do tend to take up more than our share of the seats at these types of events, but I know how much the girls love being part of a big family. I'm sorry your mom was out of town this weekend. I think she would have enjoyed it."

"She would have come, but since she plans to be with us for Thanksgiving, she wanted to have an early Thanksgiving with my aunts and uncles this weekend."

"That's understandable."

Kyle helped me into the car and then walked around to the driver's side. He pulled out of the parking lot and into traffic. My stomach knotted when we passed the rubble that had been left by the explosion that destroyed the lives of so many of my friends. The walls that had remained after the explosion had been torn down, but the site still looked like a war zone.

"I'm not sure I'm ever going to be able to drive past this spot and not feel like throwing up," I said.

Kyle blew out a breath. "Yeah. I know what you are saying. I drove over and really looked at the place a few days ago. As I stood staring at what was left of the building I had spent so much of my time in, it struck me how amazing it was that while the town offices and the council chambers are totally destroyed, the bank next door and the sheriff's office directly behind are barely damaged."

The fact that the explosion was as contained as it was really hadn't struck me as odd until right now, but Kyle was right, the explosion did seem to have been controlled, which indicated to me that the person who planted the bomb knew what they were doing. If Harriet did have the bomb in her purse, as the investigator suspected, then there would have been no way the bomber would be able to control the situation to the degree it seemed he had. Something seemed wrong with the scenario as currently presented, and I said as much to Kyle. "So what if the investigator was wrong about the bomb being in Harriet's purse? What if the bomb was in the drawer where she placed her purse, not in her purse? What if the bomber intended to destroy the building but not to kill anyone? In any other circumstance, the building would have been deserted at six o'clock."

Kyle pulled onto the lake road that led to his estate. "If that is true, then it is likely that we are barking up the wrong tree in terms of suspects."

"I agree. If Harriet was the intended victim, then looking at the victims of her blog as potential suspects makes sense, but if the intended victim really was the infrastructure all along, then those hurt by the blog really don't come into play."

Kyle pulled up in front of his house. I slipped out the passenger side door while Kyle headed up to the house to open the front door and let Echo and Trooper out. Kyle and I stood on the deck and watched as they ran up and down the beach.

"Okay," I asked after a minute. "If the building itself was the intended victim rather than the occupants of the building, then who, out of everyone we've looked at so far, do we still suspect?"

"I don't know. Maybe the heavily secured file will provide a clue. Maybe we should head inside and see if my program was able to get through the security."

"It's cold out here anyway." I whistled to Echo, who seemed to have been having fun but responded immediately.

Once we returned to the house, Kyle checked his phone for messages. There was one from Roy, so he called him back. "I'm going to put the phone on speaker, so we can both listen in," Kyle said once Roy picked up.

"Hey, Roy. It's Tj. Did you find anything?"

"I think I might have. I did some checking after my very odd conversation with Kate relating to the assertion that she'd attacked a woman named Jackie Leman. The copy of the police file Harriet had in her personal files which related to the incident is not part of Kate's employee file. In fact, it isn't part of any file that I could find. It is as if the assault never occurred."

I frowned. "Maybe it didn't. Maybe the file Harriet had is a fake."

"Initially, I thought that might be true, so I did some digging, and I managed to find a current cellphone number for Jackie. She agreed to speak to me over the phone. She confirmed that Kate had indeed attacked her, and at the time, she had been arrested. Jackie told me that Kate blamed her for the death of her father. She also assured me that, while she was at the scene where Kate's father was shot, she was in no way responsible for what happened to the man. After I spoke to Jackie, I did some additional research. I may be wrong, and all I have at this point is hearsay and not proof, but it appears that Kate used family connections to make the police file relating to her assault of Jackie Leman disappear."

"Family connections?" Kyle asked.

"Not only was Kate's dad a cop who died in the line of duty, but two of her uncles are high ranking detectives, and another of her uncles is a judge. In other words, she is connected."

"So how did Harriet find out about the assault if Kate's file, and I imagine her police record, were scrubbed?" I asked.

"I don't know."

"So are you saying that you think Kate blew up the town hall?" I asked.

"No. I don't think she was behind the bomb. I think that Harriet figured out a way to get private information that no one else seemed to have and that she used that information to tell truths others did not want to be told. I think her blog was hurtful and spiteful. I think that Kate realized that her career was on the line, but I have to believe that even if Kate had decided to eliminate Harriet, which is not what I'm saying she would have done, but even if she had come to such a conclusion, she wouldn't have risked so many innocent lives."

"Does Kate know that you know all this?" I asked.

"I'm really not sure what she knows. What I do know is that Kate is MIA. She is no longer answering her phone, and I spoke to her mother who said she took off and she has no idea where she is."

I glanced at Kyle whose brows were knit so tightly as to create a valley. "How did Harriet find out all this information?" he asked. "Sure some of it could have come from observation or local gossip, but if Kate had somehow managed to have her arrest and all traces of her arrest scrubbed, how on earth did

Harriet find out about it?"

"I don't know," Roy admitted. "And now that Harriet is gone, we may never know. What I do know is that Kate is going to be in a lot of trouble once she is tracked down. I'm sure her career is over, and I have to admit I feel sad about that. I don't know if Jackie Leman contributed to the death of Kate's father as Kate seems to think, or if Kate was misinformed as to what had gone down. And I don't know why Kate attacked her. I suppose she might have been provoked. If that is true, I don't even blame her for that. But if she found a way to scrub her file and erase her arrest, and then lied to pursue a career in law enforcement, then that is all on her."

I had to agree with Roy. It sounded like Kate might have started out as a sympathetic character, but in the end, she had made a choice, and that choice had changed things.

"So, what now?" I asked.

"The sheriff has been notified. Kate will need to face what she has done. Still, in spite of the fact that Harriet and her gossip rag threatened something Kate cared about very much, I still don't think she is our bomber."

"I don't either," Kyle agreed.

After we hung up with Roy, Kyle logged onto his computer. We decided it was best to go over everything again. We pulled out all the notes related to the explosion we'd developed to date, including the suspect list we had compiled. We decided to make a second list which only contained those suspects who would fit a scenario where the bomb had been in Harriet's desk and not in her purse. We both felt that if the bomb was placed in the desk and had been set to blow after everyone had gone home, then more likely than not, the intended target was the building, or more likely, the contents of the building. Of course, if the bomber really had intended to destroy the building and only the building, why not simply set the bomb to go off at two in the morning. Why six o'clock when there would be people still out and about? And why on Halloween when more people than usual were on the street? That part of the scenario didn't fit our new paradigm where the building or its contents were the intended victim, but Kyle and I decided to explore that option anyway.

"Okay, so I have eliminated all the blog victims from the suspect list with the exception of Kate," Kyle said.

"Yeah, it does seem as if something is going on there."

"We should also add Deputy DuPont. We haven't been able to confirm that he argued with Harriet on the day prior to the explosion, but I see no reason to think Margie would have lied."

"I agree." I glanced at the list and paused to roll this new information around in my head for a while. "While I think it is significant that the blast seemed to have been so controlled, we do need to remember that Harriet's home office was tossed. If the bomb had been placed in her desk drawer and not her purse, and the intended victim was the building and not the woman whose desk the bomb was planted in, then why was her home broken into?"

"Good question. It does seem that something isn't adding up. For every theory that we've come up with, there seems to be a piece of the puzzle that doesn't quite fit that theory." Kyle leaned back in his chair. He closed his eyes and let out a long breath. "I'm exhausted, and this is complicated. What do you say we call it a night and pick this up tomorrow?"

"I'm good with that. My brain is pretty fried at this point. Did you ever check to see if the program you left running was able to get into the heavily secured file?"

"It looks like the program is eighty percent of the way there. I'm sure we'll be able to get in by tomorrow. I keep hoping that whatever Harriet had locked away will give us the clue we need to figure this whole thing out."

# CHAPTER 24

Saturday, November 18

As it turned out, the program Kyle had left running had managed to get into the file by the following morning. Inside were several documents including a missing persons report from eighteen years ago, a police report relating to a woman who had been arrested for drug trafficking, a contract for a large amount of concrete that appeared to have been poured eighteen years ago, and some scribbles in Harriet's handwriting that, at this point, made no sense to either of us.

"The missing persons report in the file is associated with a man named Robert Edmonton," Kyle explained to Jenna and me after joining us in his kitchen where we'd been going over our plans for the food for Thanksgiving.

Jenna sat forward slightly, wrapping her hands around her mug of coffee. "I remember hearing about this. Robert Edmonton owned the Serenity Community Bank. He was last seen at the bank where he planned to work late. He never came home, so his wife filed a missing persons report, and the whole town set out to look for him, thinking he had met with foul play. He never did show up, but it was later discovered that a large amount of cash was missing from the vault. Once the cash was found to be missing, the popular opinion changed from possible abduction to midlife crisis, which most assumed played out with the man stealing from his own bank and taking off."

"Robert Edmonton went missing a long time ago. We were still in high school. How do you remember all of this?" I asked.

"My dad was good friends with Edmonton. His disappearance hit both my parents hard. I remember that my parents and their friends spent a lot of time debating the different theories as to what had most likely occurred. There were those who thought he'd taken off, which seemed to be what the sheriff and his team thought, and then there were those who figured he was dead."

"Okay, so what does this mean?" I asked. "Are we thinking the explosion at the town hall is in some way associated with this missing person?"

Kyle shrugged. "I have no idea. I really don't see how it could relate unless Harriet stumbled across evidence that Edmonton hadn't simply taken off, but had been murdered. That would be a juicy tidbit for her blog, even if the murder occurred almost two decades ago."

"Okay, say that Harriet had some sort of proof that Edmonton had been murdered and was planning to expose this truth. Say the killer somehow discovered Harriet's plan and decided to stop her. Why blow up an entire building?" Jenna asked. "The one question we keep coming back to is if Harriet was the intended victim, why not just shoot her or stab her or poison her?"

That, I decided was a good question. An individual, any individual, as the intended victim didn't really make sense when the fact was that an entire structure was demolished.

Kyle's phone buzzed. It was Roy, so he put the phone on speaker. "Jenna and Tj are here with me," Kyle informed the deputy.

"Good morning, everyone," Roy responded.

"Any news on either the missing persons report or the arrest record?" Kyle asked.

Roy shared what he knew about the missing person, which basically mirrored what Jenna had just told us.

"And the woman who was arrested?"

"Her name is Julie Matheson. She was arrested just two weeks after Robert Edmonton turned up missing. It appears to me that her police record has been tampered with."

"Tampered with?" I asked.

"Based on my knowledge of what should be included in an arrest report, there is information missing. Quite a bit of it actually. Based on what does appear in the report, it seems that Ms. Matheson was arrested for drug trafficking after a very large amount of cocaine was found in her apartment. I went back through the court transcripts and found multiple statements where Ms. Matheson claimed that the cocaine did not belong to her, and had been planted, as part of a setup. The DA wasn't buying her story since she had several previous arrests for drug possession in smaller amounts. He argued for a maximum sentence, and she spent fifteen years in prison."

"Do you have a photo of the woman?" I asked.

"Yeah. I'll forward it to your phone."

I pulled up the photo. "Black hair, brown eyes, long thin scar over her right eye." I looked at Kyle. "Does that ring a bell?"

"The woman Harriet had lunch with on the day she died."

"Exactly."

"Okay, so Harriet had lunch with Julie Matheson on the day she and the entire town hall was blown to smithereens. Are we thinking this woman is the one who gave Harriet the bomb?" Jenna asked.

"Actually," I answered, "our current theory is that the bomb was not in Harriet's purse as we first thought, but in the drawer where she kept her purse."

Jenna raised a brow. "So Harriet wasn't the intended victim?"

"We can't know for certain at this point, but given the precision of the explosion, we are thinking the bomb must have been placed in a stationary location. Putting it in Harriet's purse would be too random," I informed her.

"So the intended victim was the building. Why?" Jenna asked.

"We don't know yet," I admitted.

"The series of events really is confusing," Roy agreed. "The precision with which the building was blown up really does point the theory that the intended victim was the building itself. And the fact that the explosion was so precise, also leads to the idea that the person who set the bomb was very skilled at what they did. I think we have to assume that the bomb was set at some point in time before the date of the explosion; otherwise, someone would have seen the bomber poking around in the building. If that were the case, the emergency meeting would not have been called when the bomb was planted, so I think we have to assume the bomber did not anticipate any human casualties."

"So why six p.m. on Halloween?" Jenna asked. "Why not midnight?"

"I don't know," Roy answered. "At this point, there is a lot I don't know."

"Like why Harriet had lunch with this ex-con, and if that lunch and the presence of Julie Matheson's arrest record in Harriet's file are in any way related to the explosion at the town hall," I added.

I sat back and tried to understand why Harriet would seek out Julie Matheson. I assumed she had been the one doing the seeking. Julie had been out of prison for close to three years, so it made no sense that she would come looking for Harriet at this point. I would suspect that Harriet planned to do a blog on Julie and her arrest, but as far as I knew, Harriet hadn't spoken to any of her blog subjects ahead of time, so that theory really didn't make sense. Perhaps Julie had information Harriet needed about someone she had planned to write about. It didn't seem that a missing bank president and a convicted drug dealer would be linked, but both reports were found in the same file on Harriet's computer, so in my mind, there had to be a connection.

"Who filled out the missing persons report?" Kyle asked Roy.

"Deputy DuPont."

"Why DuPont? I thought he worked out of the office in Indulgence."

"I'd have to check to know for certain, but he would have been relatively new to the force eighteen years ago, so he may have started in the Serenity office, or he may have just been in the North Shore office to fill in if someone was on vacation, or out on medical leave."

"And who was the person responsible for arresting Julie Matheson?" Kyle asked.

"Deputy DuPont," Roy answered.

"His name does seem to keep coming up," I said.

"It does at that," Roy agreed.

"I think we need to talk to this woman," Kyle said. "Do you have an address?"

"I do. I'll call her and see if she is willing to speak to us voluntarily. If not, I can go through legal channels. Once I get ahold of her, I'll call you back."

After the Roy hung up, Jenna and I decided to go into town to order flowers for Thanksgiving, as well as linens that matched since we were going to need to utilize at least four large tables. We decided on tablecloths the color of dark sand and napkins in a chocolate brown. Rita had a good selection of flowers on order for holiday arrangements, so we ordered a fall bouquet for each table and arranged to pick them up on Wednesday. Once we had linens and flowers ordered, we headed to the holiday shop for other items to use as decorations for the house. Initially, I wasn't going to fuss with all that, but Jenna's enthusiasm was rubbing off on me. By the time we returned to Kyle's from shopping, I was the most excited I'd been about hosting the holiday than I'd been so far.

"Roy called shortly after you left," Kyle said to Jenna and me after we walked in from the driveway.

"Did he have news about Julie Matheson?" I asked.

"Not about Julie Matheson, but I guess the crime scene guys were at the blast site this morning with high tech equipment they hoped would uncover clues they may have missed the first time around."

"And did they find something?"

Kyle nodded. "A body."

I frowned. I glanced at Jenna. She was frowning as well. "A body?" I asked.

"Buried in the concrete," Kyle specified. "A tiny part of it was exposed by the blast, so they dug the rest of it up. It appears as if it has been there since the foundation was poured."

"You're kidding?" I gasped.

Kyle shook his head. "I'm afraid not. The skeleton is being processed, but quite coincidentally, they think it might be Robert Edmonton."

"We find a file relating to Edmonton's disappearance eighteen years ago, and then a few hours later, his body is found? What are the odds?" Jenna asked.

"Astronomically unlikely," I answered. "Still, I suppose that finding Edmonton's body fits with everything else we've uncovered."

"So Robert Edmonton did meet with foul play," Jenna shook her head slightly as she set the bag she carried on the kitchen counter. "My dad never did believe that he stole money from his own bank and then took off after suffering some sort of midlife crisis."

"Were there any clues as to how Edmonton ended up in the concrete?" I asked.

"The crime scene guys are still looking into things, but Roy did some checking, and the concrete that served as the foundation for the new town hall was poured two days after Edmonton was last seen."

"So someone knew the foundation was going to be poured and took advantage of it," Jenna said.

"We think there was more going on than that," Kyle answered. "It turns out that the concrete for the town hall wasn't due to be poured until the following week, but Mayor Wallaby arranged for the concrete to be poured early. The cost for this early pour was an additional twenty percent, which says to me that Wallaby was in on whatever occurred that led to the president of the local bank being killed and buried in the foundation of the town hall."

I am pretty sure my mouth was hanging open at this point, although I have no idea why I was so surprised. On more than one occasion, Wallaby had demonstrated that he was very willing to operate outside the confines of the law.

"So Wallaby was in on the whole thing," Jenna voiced the thought I'd been having.

"It looks like Wallaby was involved in some manner," Kyle confirmed. "As of the last time I spoke to Roy, he had not been able to get ahold of Julie Matheson, but he had been able to get ahold of her defense attorney. He told Roy that he had never believed Julie was guilty of the charges against her, and it was his conviction that she had been set up as she maintained all along. He told Roy that Julie had seen a man carrying what looked to be a dead body on the night Edmonton was last seen. It was dark, and she'd been unable to say with certainty who the man was, but she was fairly certain the man carrying the body was Deputy DuPont. She told Mayor Wallaby as much since she was afraid to go to anyone in law enforcement based on what she'd seen, and the next thing she knew, she was being arrested."

"Why would DuPont kill Edmonton?" Jenna asked.

"I don't know," I admitted. "But if DuPont did kill Edmonton, that would be huge news, even now, Harriet must have somehow found out what happened and planned to reveal the cover-up in her blog. She must have needed to confirm some details, so she asked Julie to lunch." I paused to work through the logistics of the whole thing. "It really does make sense if you stop to think about it. If DuPont killed Edmonton for some reason and then enlisted Wallaby's help in covering it up, Harriet might even have known the truth all this time. She was famous for listening in on Wallaby's conversations, and even snooping through his files."

"If she knew all along, why wait so long to tell what she knew?" Kyle asked.

"She just recently took on the role as gatekeeper for the truth," Jenna pointed out. "Prior to Judge Harper dying and Harriet creating Sinful Secrets, she appeared to be the keeper of as many secrets as anyone, but she kept them to herself for the most part. Once she came to the conclusion that secrets were bad, she began to reveal confidences she had previously kept close to her chest."

"So how does Harriet deciding to rat out Deputy DuPont after all this time relate to the town hall being blown up?" I asked. "Are we thinking DuPont blew it up? Because that actually makes no sense. If he wanted Harriet dead, it seems that he would have killed her in a manner that wouldn't have risked exposing the body he'd buried all those years ago."

No one spoke for a moment, and then Kyle jumped in. "Roy told me that Julie told her attorney that when she went to Wallaby with her assertion that there was a body buried in the foundation of the town hall, he pointed out that the only way to prove or disprove that assertion was to tear up the foundation, which he was unwilling to do. It makes sense that Julie might have blown up the building, or had the building blown up, in order to expose the body that she knew had been buried there eighteen years ago."

"Yeah," I said, with doubt evident in my voice. "That could have been what happened, but I don't think so. If Julie was going to blow up the building to prove that she had seen what she'd sworn she had, why wait so long? She has been out of prison for a while now."

"And if Julie was behind this whole thing, why trash Harriet's home office?" Jenna added. "Harriet had lunch with Julie on the day of the explosion. If she had been planning to blow up the town hall, it seems as if Harriet had been willing to work with her."

"There is something that still isn't fitting quite right," Kyle admitted.

"We don't know exactly when Harriet's home office was trashed," I added. "It could have been a day or more after the explosion. Maybe after Harriet died, Julie went looking for the proof Harriet said she had, or maybe someone else, such as DuPont, wanted to suppress what Harriet knew."

"Hold on," Jenna said. "Are we saying that either Julie or Harriet planted the bomb? Because that makes no sense. Not if they were working together in an effort to expose the fact that a body actually was buried in the foundation of the town hall, which I think is where this discussion is going. First of all,

Harriet would never agree to blow up the town hall. It was like her second home. And even if Julie did convince her it was the only way, why would she agree to the emergency meeting? At the very least, you would think she would make up a reason for the meeting to be delayed until the following day. She could even have used the holiday as an excuse for the delay."

"Actually," Kyle said, "if, as we suspect, the meeting was called by Lloyd to inform the group of the lawsuit from James Kingston, it seems like Harriet would have scheduled the meeting for the next day anyway. It wasn't like the potential of a lawsuit was so important as to disturb everyone's Halloween."

"Had Harriet ever called a same day meeting before?" I asked.

"Once," Kyle answered. "But she sent out emails in the morning about a meeting to be held that evening. The emails were worded to give the recipient the option of attending or not. The text on Halloween had more urgency to it, and a lawsuit that hadn't yet been filed would not, in my mind, constitute the sort of urgency indicated by the text. When I first saw the letter from Kingston, I was sure that the lawsuit was the reason the meeting was called, but at this point, I'm less certain."

"So if not the lawsuit, what?" I asked.

Kyle slowly shook his head. "I don't know. No one alive seems to know. I'm beginning to wonder if we'll ever know."

"So, what now?" I asked.

"I know we can't figure out how the body in the foundation is related to the town hall being blown up, but it seems it has to be linked in some way," Jenna pointed out. "It would just be too bizarre if it wasn't. I will agree that there doesn't seem to be a logical sequence of events that explains everything, but that doesn't mean there isn't one we just haven't stumbled across yet."

"I do feel like there are still pieces of information that need to be discovered if we are ever going to stitch the entire picture together," I agreed.

"It would help if we could definitively determine if the emergency meeting was intended to get the town council there for the purpose of blowing up the council along with the town hall, or if the explosion and the meeting were oddly unrelated," Kyle pointed out.

# CHAPTER 25

Tuesday, November 21

Jenna and I decided to do all our Thanksgiving shopping on Tuesday in order to beat the Wednesday crowd. Of course, the store seemed almost as crowded today as it had last time when we'd shopped on the Wednesday before Thanksgiving, but we vowed to keep our wits in spite of the chaos and power through until we'd picked up every single item on the list.

"Are you okay?" I asked Jenna.

"I'm fine. Why do you ask?"

"You just look a little... I don't know... something."

"I'm fine," Jenna assured me. "I guess I didn't sleep all that well, and I have a bit of a headache. I'm thinking I should up my pie count by a few," Jenna said, heading toward the apples. "Several people have been added to the guest list since I did my original count."

"Do we have enough pumpkin?" I asked.

Jenna nodded. "I think we are set for pumpkin. I remember someone liking cherry, so I might make one of those as well as an extra apple."

"Exactly how many pies are you making?"

"A bunch," Jenna answered. "With so many guests, I'm sure you'll have a need for leftovers, and to be honest, now that I've sold the restaurant, I really miss cooking for a crowd."

Jenna paused when we reached the dairy aisle. She took her phone out of her pocket and looked at the display. "It's Dennis. He is at the ice rink with Kari and Gracie. He wanted to let me know that Rosalie came by and picked up Ashley and Kristi. I guess she is taking them to Reno to get fabric for the jackets they are going to make this week."

"That's nice of her. Ashley is really excited about the jacket she has planned to match the purse Rosalie helped the girls to make a couple weekends ago."

Jenna began loading whipping cream in the cart. "I'm impressed. You actually managed to say that without sounding annoyed or jealous."

I shrugged. "I think I'm over the queen bee thing we talked about. When I told Rosalie that Kyle and I were engaged, she was happy for me, but I could see that she was upset that the girls and I would be moving out. I guess in the back of my mind, I'd always assumed that she wouldn't want us living at the resort once she moved in, which made me feel pushed out, but I can see that I was wrong. She has worked hard to make it work for all of us, and I am determined to do so as well."

"Good for you. Should we get ice cream for the fruit pies?"

I picked up a dozen eggs. "Sure. I guess so. We'll grab that last so that it doesn't melt." I looked toward the bakery aisle. "I was going to pick up some extra rolls for sandwiches and leftovers, but it looks like Armageddon over there."

"Rosalie is baking rolls. I suppose you can just ask her to make extra," Jenna suggested.

"I'll do that. She seems anxious to be part of this, so I don't think she'll mind. Should we buy extra gravy for the leftovers?"

Jenna hemmed and hawed, and offered several solutions.

"So did you talk to Dennis about tree cutting on Saturday?" I asked Jenna after she'd put several cans of gravy in the cart.

"I haven't had a chance to talk to him. He's been really busy. In fact, given our schedules, we haven't had the chance to talk at all other than by text or phone messages. But I'm sure we're in. He worked last night, but now he'll be off until next Monday barring a real emergency."

"I'm glad he is off for the weekend. It seems like he has been working a lot of shifts."

"They've been shorthanded, so he has been covering his duties as Captain and covering part of the shift work."

The poor guy was going to work himself into an early grave if he wasn't careful. "Did you talk to your mom about Saturday?"

"Mom wants Dennis and me to pick up a tree for their place. She didn't want Bookman to overdo, and it seems like tree cutting day is always a long and labor-intensive day no matter how simple we try to make it."

I followed Jenna as she headed toward the aisle with the olives and pickles. "Kyle and I discussed the fact that we were going to be low on muscle this year. My dad can't help out, and Kyle isn't supposed to lift anything over fifteen pounds. You and I and Dennis can cut and carry, and I suppose if Bree and Pastor Dan come, they can help as well. I thought I might try to grab a couple of staff members to come along this year if anyone is in town. The resort reopens the week following Thanksgiving weekend, so I imagine that Logan and Noah will have returned from their time off."

"We could just get the trees from a lot," Jenna suggested.

"We could. And we could just buy frozen pies."

The look of horror on Jenna's face convinced me that she had gotten my point about the importance of the Jensen family tree cutting tradition.

"Maybe we can cut the trees for all the residences, and you can ask Noah to oversee the trees for the resort," Jenna suggested. "I'm afraid our tree cutting crew has suffered more than their share of casualties this year, and I'm not sure that cutting so many trees is realistic."

I hated to admit it, but I supposed Jenna was right. "I'll call Dad and talk to him about it. I suppose he may already have made arrangements for the trees for the lodge, restaurant, and cabins. I assumed we'd go out as a family and get them like we usually do, but given his physical limitations, Dad may have made other plans."

After we completed our shopping, we stopped at Kyle's to drop off the food that wasn't related to the pies Jenna was planning to make. He was on the phone when we arrived, so I stuck my head in his office to let him know we were there, and then I joined Jenna in the kitchen to help put the food away. I supposed in some ways we may have gone completely overboard, but the last thing I wanted was to run out of some key ingredient on Thanksgiving Day with a houseful of friends and family.

"So are you still planning to announce your engagement at Thanksgiving?" Jenna asked as she stacked canned goods in the pantry.

"I'm not sure. The family knows, and that's the most important thing. I don't mind letting everyone else know, but it has occurred to me that once the masses know, people will start asking about a date."

"And you aren't ready to set a date?"

"Not really. I promised Ashley and Gracie that we wouldn't do anything until we worked everything out relating to the living arrangements. Kyle and I talked about it and came to the conclusion that we should wait and see how things naturally develop."

"Are you considering options other than you and the girls moving in here with Kyle?"

I blew out a breath. "I don't know. Maybe. I'm not sure. It's complicated."

Jenna gave me a quick, hard hug. "Just take your time. As you said, the odds are that things will unfold naturally. I can't see that anything will be gained in forcing things before you are ready. I know you have known Kyle for a long time, but you have only been a couple for five months. Less than five months actually."

That seemed like a switch from her previous advice to tell the girls how it was going to be and not let them sway me. I glanced at Jenna. She seemed different today. Almost more emotional. I wondered if she and Dennis were involved in another of their increasingly frequent spats. "I guess it is true that Kyle and I haven't really been a couple all that long, and Kyle seems fine with taking things slow, so I guess, at this point, that is what we will do. I'm still thinking about a summer or fall wedding, but I guess we'll see how it all comes together."

"I'm not sure we are going to have room in the freezer for all the ice cream we bought," Jenna said.

"Kyle has an extra freezer in the walk-in pantry."

Jenna opened the door and walked inside the pantry that was really the size of a room. "I never realized that was a freezer," Jenna called out to me. "The way he has it built in, it looks like a cabinet. I have to say I am officially jealous."

"When Kyle remodeled the kitchen, he went all out to make sure everything was perfect," I had to agree.

I looked up as Kyle walked into the room from the main living area. He had a frown on his face. "Problem?" I asked.

"I'm not sure. That was Roy on the phone. Apparently, he was able to get ahold of Wallaby, who is currently living in New Jersey. Wallaby was willing to share what he knew in return for full immunity for his part in what went down. It took some doing, but Roy was able to arrange that."

"And?" I asked. I glanced at Jenna, who'd emerged from the

pantry and joined me.

"According to Roy, Wallaby had been approached by Julie Matheson as she claimed. She told him that she'd seen someone who she thought might have been Deputy DuPont carrying something which looked to be a human body wrapped up in a blanket. Wallaby promised Matheson that he would look into things. And he did. He called DuPont and shared with him what Matheson had told him. DuPont admitted that he had shot Edmonton, but that it had been an accident. He'd gone by the sheriff's office to pick up something he had left behind and had noticed the back door to the bank was ajar. He was off duty, but he figured that a robbery was in progress, so he grabbed his gun and went to check it out. He saw a man dressed in black inside the vault room. The room was dark other than a dim light over the door to the vault, so he hadn't been able to identify the intruder. He called for him to freeze, but the man tried to run. DuPont told Wallaby that he aimed his gun and shot at him, intending to injure, not kill him. It was only after he realized the man was dead that he recognized the thief as the bank president."

"It sounds like an accident. Why cover it up?" I asked.

"Wallaby told Roy that DuPont had told him that he'd been off duty, and had actually had quite a bit to drink when the incident went down. He knew that due to his level of intoxication, he would be held accountable for what happened whether the shooting was called for or not."

"So why did Edmonton try to run?" Jenna asked.

"DuPont said he had a bag filled with money," Kyle answered. "It appeared as if he actually was planning to rob his own bank. DuPont didn't know why."

"So how did Julie end up in jail?" I asked.

"Roy said that Wallaby told him that he and DuPont came up with the plan to have the concrete for the town hall poured early. They hid the body beneath some beams so that the workmen pouring the concrete wouldn't notice it. Once the concrete hardened, all traces of Robert Edmonton were erased forever. When it became apparent, however, that Julie Matheson wasn't going to leave the whole thing alone, DuPont planted the drugs and then arrested her."

"And Julie? Has Roy been able to track her down?"

Kyle shook his head. "She hasn't been home, and she hasn't shown up at her place of employment since the explosion. I suppose that could lead to the theory that she was the one to blow up the town hall so the skeleton would be found and her story would be proven, but it seems like there are still a lot of unanswered questions even if she does turn out to be the one who planted the bomb."

"Yeah like why the emergency meeting that led to the death of two people was called in the first place," I added.

"Or whether Harriet knew the bomb was in the building when she called the emergency meeting," Jenna joined in.

"I'm not sure how we will ever know that."

Jenna and I headed over to her house after we finished putting away everything at Kyle's. She planned to start the pies, and I planned to sit and chat with her while she baked. Dennis had gone to the hardware store, Gracie and Kari were playing upstairs, and Rosalie was still entertaining Ashley and Kristi. It had been a long time since I'd sat and chatted with Jenna while she cooked, and I found that I'd missed it. When Jenna had owned The Antiquery, I'd stop by and sit and chat with her while she cooked all the time. Things had changed in the past year. I wasn't unhappy with the way things were now, but I would admit to feeling just a bit of nostalgia for the way things had once been.

"Is your headache still bothering you?" I asked. "You seem sort of off today. If you aren't feeling well, we can buy the pies from the bakery."

"I feel fine." Jenna tied her apron around her waist. "But I do have something to tell you," Jenna said, somewhat hesitantly, after turning on the oven to preheat.

I paused at the serious tone in Jenna's voice. "Something bad?"

Jenna stopped what she was doing and frowned. "To be honest, I'm not really sure if I would consider my news good or bad. The only term I can come up with at this point is unexpected." Her smile, which had seemed forced from the beginning, faded just a bit. "Totally and completely unexpected."

I crossed the room and took Jenna's hand. "It's okay. Whatever it is. We'll figure it out."

"Thanks." Jenna wiped a tear from her eye.

"Are you sick? Is one of the kids sick? Is it Dennis? Are you getting a divorce?"

Jenna's head snapped up. "Divorce? Why would you even suggest that?"

I shrugged. "I don't know. I know that your marriage has been experiencing some growing pains in the past few months since Dennis made Captain, and his role at work changed, and you sold The Antiquery, and your role in life changed. You just look so scared, and divorce was where my mind ended up."

"Dennis and I are fine. Yes, I will admit that his promotion has caused a level of stress that we weren't anticipating, and my selling the restaurant has left me feeling sort of lost, but I love Dennis, and he loves me. In spite of whatever little bumps we face along the way, we will always be okay."

I blew out a breath. "That's good. I'm glad to hear that." I squeezed Jenna's hand. "So if no one is sick and your marriage is fine, what is it?"

"I'm pregnant."

Okay, I hadn't seen that coming. "Pregnant?"

Jenna nodded.

"Are you sure?"

She nodded again.

I smiled and hugged my best friend. "That's great." I pulled back just a bit and studied Jenna's face. "That is great? Right?"

Jenna started to sob. "I don't know. I guess I haven't had time to process everything yet. I will say that having another child at this point in my life was not at all on the radar. Kristi is in junior high, and Kari only has a few years of elementary school left. After Dennis made Captain and I decided to sell the restaurant, we began to discuss what our lives would look like after we got both kids off to college. We even started a special savings account. We were going to finally go to Paris and Rome and all the wonderful places I've only been able to dream of to this point. But now..."

"Now you will have a brand-new baby to love. That has to be better than a trip to pretty much anywhere."

Jenna wiped her arm across her face to dry her eyes. "I know you are right, and I know I will love this baby, but I guess I need some time to get used to the idea. Kari is almost nine. She will be close to ten when the baby is born. That is just such a big gap."

I hugged Jenna again. "It is a pretty big gap, but it will be fine. You'll see." I handed Jenna a tissue.

She blew her nose. "I guess."

"What does Dennis think?"

Jenna cringed.

"Was he mad?" I narrowed my gaze. "He wasn't mad, was he?"

"Actually, I haven't told him yet."

I gasped. "Haven't told him? Why not?"

"I just took the pregnancy test this morning. He was still at work when I took the test and when he got home, I thought about pulling him aside before I left to meet you for shopping, but Ashley and Gracie were here, and I guess I just needed to get used to the idea before I had the strength to deal with whatever volatile emotions another child might bring about."

I frowned. "You don't think he will be happy?"

Jenna shook her head. "I'm not sure he will be. I know he is only thirty-four years old, but he already has thirteen years with the department. He will be eligible to retire with partial benefits when he is forty and full benefits when he is fifty. Even earlier if we buy down the time, which we have talked about doing. I realize retirement is a way down the road but still close enough for him to think about it from time to time. I'm just not sure how he is going to feel about starting over again with a baby."

"It wasn't all that long ago when the two of you wanted a baby very much," I reminded her.

"A lot has changed in the past few years."

I supposed a lot had changed. For all of us.

"Let's just get back to the pies," Jenna suggested. "I really should talk to Dennis before I say anything else. I really should have told him first, but when you asked how I was doing, I found myself blurting it out."

"Okay. Let's get back to the pies, but if you want to talk, just call me. Any time, day or night."

"Okay. I appreciate that."

"I wonder if we are going to have enough chocolate. Everyone loves the pumpkin, but it seems like it is the chocolate we usually run out of."

Jenna baked, and I chatted about anything and everything that I could think of that wouldn't remind her about the news she needed to have time to process and deal with. Jenna's fear that she might be past the stage in her life where she wanted to start with a new baby had me wondering if I was past the stage in my own life where I wanted to start with an infant as well. I supposed it would behoove me to really stop and look at how my life, as well as the lives of Ashley and Gracie, would be affected with the introduction of a new baby, which I knew in my heart, Kyle wanted very much, and I was sure, assumed we'd have.

# CHAPTER 26

Halfway through the pies, Jenna realized she was low on sugar. I volunteered to run into town and pick some up. Knowing how crowded the market would be, I decided to stop at the local liquor store, which also had a small mini-mart attached. I figured I could get the sugar there and avoid the crowd. As I passed the aisle with the whiskey, I saw a woman I was sure was the woman Roy had been looking for. "Julie?" I asked. "Are you Julie Matheson?"

The woman scowled. "How did you find me?"

"I didn't find you so much as ran into you. I'm here for sugar."

The woman turned back toward the whiskey selection.

"Do you know that Deputy Fisher has been looking for you? He has some questions. We all do."

"I know. I obviously chose not to be interviewed."

"Look," I tried. "Two of my friends died in that blast. Others were injured. If you know anything..."

The woman turned and looked at me. "I'm sorry about what happened to Harriet, and I'm sorry about the fact that others were killed and injured, but the last time I tried to do the right thing, I ended up in prison for fifteen years."

"I know. And that was awful. I totally understand why you don't trust cops. Would you talk to me? Just me?"

The woman didn't respond.

"Please. I really only have a few questions. It won't take long."

"Okay. I'm living in a monthly motel a couple doors down." She handed me a large bottle. "Buy this for me, and we can chat."

I happily agreed to the purchase of the whiskey, and then followed Julie to a dive motel that I'd been campaigning to tear down for quite some time. I supposed if you didn't want to be found, it was as good a place as any to hide out. I knew the motel owner didn't bother to ask for ID and was happy to take cash for payment. After we entered her room, Julie pointed toward a chair and indicated that I should sit down.

"Okay. So what do you want to know?" she asked.

"Did you blow up the town hall?"

"No."

"But you do know something about the town hall being destroyed?"

"I do."

"Okay," I tried to ignore the stench of cigarette smoke and focus on the conversation. "Why don't you tell me what you know?"

The woman got up. She began to pace around the room. I could see that she was nervous. I guess I didn't blame her.

"I assume, based on what you've said, that you know what happened eighteen years ago," Julie started off.

"I know some of what happened. I know that you saw Deputy DuPont carrying a body which turned out to belong to Robert Edmonton, and I know that you told Mayor Wallaby what you'd seen, only to end up being arrested for a crime you didn't commit."

"That's right. Do you know I had a daughter, a little girl named Amelia, who was taken from me after my arrest? Do you know that during the fifteen years I was in prison, she grew up thinking I was guilty of the charges against me? Do you know that my baby grew to hate me, and even though I am out of prison, and have tried to connect with her, she refuses to take my calls?"

"I didn't know any of that," I admitted.

"I will admit that I wasn't always an upstanding citizen. I got into quite a bit of trouble when I was younger. I was even arrested a few times. Nothing huge, but I had a record. But then, I got pregnant with Amelia, and I knew I needed to clean up my act. I got a job, and I rented a fairly decent apartment. I might have started out rough, but by the time Wallaby and DuPont framed me, I had a daughter I adored and was planning a future. All of that was stripped from me. And for what? Just so some dirty cop could get off scot-free rather than facing up to what he had done?"

"I'm so sorry. I can see that you have every reason to be angry. I don't blame you for wanting to seek revenge for what was done to you, or for wanting to prove your innocence after all this time."

Julie wiped a tear from her cheek. "At first, all I could think about was getting revenge for what had been done to me," she admitted. "I even had a plan and a means of getting that revenge. But then, DuPont reached out to me on my last day in prison and told me that if I told anyone what I knew, he would make sure that I never saw my daughter again. I missed her so much and wanted her in my life, so I decided to let it go and try to rebuild with what I had."

What a snake! "But something changed recently?" I prompted.

"Yes. Harriet came to me. I guess she'd overheard Mayor Wallaby and Deputy DuPont talking all those years ago and knew the truth. Her loyalty had been to Mayor Wallaby at the time, so she never did anything about what she knew, but it seems she recently had an awakening and decided that secrets were evil, so she told me that she wanted to come clean about what she'd overheard. She wanted to be sure that what she printed about the death of Robert Edmonton was factual, so she hoped I would be willing to be interviewed. I told her I was willing to speak to her, and we arranged to get together."

"And then?" I asked.

"We met in my home. She told me what she knew, and I shared what I knew. I applauded her plan to make Deputy DuPont accountable for his crime both to Robert Edmonton and to me after all these years and told her I would support her in any way that I could. I had to hand it to the woman, she did her research and managed to dig up the proof she needed. I understand that a lot of people found her blog hurtful, but in this instance, I felt she was providing a real service to both Edmonton's family and me. I'm not sure how, but DuPont found out what Harriet was doing."

I remembered that Harriet had been seen arguing with DuPont, and I also remembered that Gina had told me that someone from the sheriff's office had hacked into the town's records. I supposed that was DuPont looking for what Harriet had. Of course, the proof she'd dug up hadn't been in the town's files, but that didn't mean he hadn't caught her when she accessed the police reports she had in her own files. "Go on," I prompted.

"DuPont told Harriet that if she published what she knew, what had happened to me would likewise happen to her."

"He was going to frame and then arrest her?" I asked.

Julie nodded. "That is what he told her. Apparently, framing people seems to be his thing. Harriet believed him, so she called me on the day of the explosion, and we met for lunch. We talked and came up with a plan. We figured if she told a bunch of people what she knew before DuPont was able to frame her, then the frame would be impossible."

"So it was Harriet who called the emergency meeting?"

Julie nodded. "She was going to share with the entire town council what she knew, and she planned to provide them with the proof she had to support her claim. Her plan was a good one, and would have worked if the bomb hadn't been planted and set off before she could tell the town council everything."

"Do you know who planted the bomb?"

"No," Julie assured me. "I don't know who did, but if I had to guess I would say it was DuPont."

"Why would he plant the bomb? The explosion revealed the existence of Robert Edmonton's remains, which seems counterproductive to his desire to keep the fate of the man under wraps."

Julie's face grew thoughtful "That's true. When I heard about the explosion, I just assumed it was him trying to prevent Harriet from telling what she knew, but I suppose the method used doesn't make sense."

"Did anyone else know the truth about what happened to Robert Edmonton? Someone other than you, Harriet, DuPont, and of course, Wallaby?"

"No, I don't think so." She furrowed her brow. "Well, maybe."

"Maybe?" I asked.

"Harriet didn't want to tell Deputy Fisher what she knew until she was able to talk to the council as a whole because she was afraid Deputy DuPont would find out what she was up to. But when we met the first time, she did say that she felt it only right that she talk to Edmonton's widow. I don't know if she had the chance to do so, but she might have."

I supposed she made as good a suspect as anyone.

After I spoke to Julie, I headed back to Jenna's. I gave her the sugar I had been sent to fetch and filled her in on my discussion with Julie. Jenna finished the pies she wanted to make today, and then we headed to Kyle's. We called Roy and told him what we had found out, and he suggested that he come over for a brainstorming session.

# CHAPTER 27

"Okay, so we now know who called the emergency meeting and why," I started off. "We know who the body in the foundation belongs to and we know how he got there. We don't know who placed the bomb in the town hall, or why they wanted to blow it up. We don't know if the bomber intended to blow up the council, or if they assumed the place would be empty when the building went kaboom."

"We also don't know why Edmonton was taking a bag of cash from his bank's vault at the time DuPont shot him if that is even what happened," Roy added. "Maybe the midlife starting over elsewhere theory wasn't all that far off. Maybe that is exactly what he would have done if DuPont hadn't shot him."

"Speaking of DuPont, do you have enough to arrest him before he has a chance to take off?" I asked.

"Based on the official statement provided by Wallaby, DuPont is currently in custody," Roy confirmed. "We are going to need to find hard evidence if we want to keep him there."

"I doubt it will be easy to find anything to prove what Wallaby told us if he doesn't have any proof of what occurred," Jenna said.

"Maybe Harriet did have proof," Kyle said. "Maybe the proof she had was the reason someone, probably DuPont, blew up the town hall."

I tilted my head just a bit. "So you think the bomber

believed that proof of what went down that night was located somewhere within the town offices, so he blew the whole thing up to destroy the proof he believed might exist?"

"It's a theory," Kyle said.

"Okay, so I assume that if DuPont blew up the building to destroy the evidence that he believed Harriet had about the night he'd killed Edmonson, then he must have been successful in doing what he intended, and the proof most likely no longer exists."

"Maybe not," Kyle said. "Wallaby had a floor safe in his office when he was mayor. I don't think there are many people who even knew of its existence. I found out after Judge Harper died, and I was looking for clues relating to his death. I know Harriet knew about the safe, but other than that, I don't know of a single soul who knew of its existence."

"I wonder if anyone has accessed the floor safe since the building was destroyed." Jenna wondered.

"It would be buried beneath the rubble at this point, but I do know that it was made of reinforced steel. I'm sure it survived the explosion," Kyle answered.

"Maybe we should check it out," Roy suggested, before offering to drive. Jenna, Kyle, and I piled into his cruiser, although of the three cars available to us, his was the least comfortable.

Shortly after we arrived at what remained of the town hall and were able to access the hidden safe beneath the rubble, we realized we'd found the rest of the story.

"Well, I'll be dammed," Roy exclaimed, as he thumbed through a file stuffed with the evidence that Harriet had somehow managed to dig up.

"James Kingston has been blackmailing people?" I gasped.

"Based on the items found in this file, it looks like he has been blackmailing people in order to obtain the land he desired, but the owners had been unwilling to sell for a long time," Roy said.

"How on earth did Harriet get ahold of this file?" I asked. I picked up one of the documents. I had to hand it to Kingston; he knew how to get what he wanted. The document I found was a purchase agreement between himself and Byron Boatman for the land where he was planning to build his condominium development along with Lloyd Benson. The land had been in the Boatman family for generations, and I'd wondered how Kingston had gotten ahold of it, but apparently, Byron had cheated on his taxes, Kingston had found proof that would probably have landed Byron in prison, so Byron had agreed to sell him the land in exchange for his silence.

"Here is a contract between Kingston and Lloyd," Kyle said. "I would say we know why Lloyd was helping Kingston with his vacation rental issue. Did you know that Lloyd illegally obtained a piece of beachfront property when he had the land surveyed and the property lines redrawn to benefit himself?"

"I'm not surprised," I said. "If you remember, he tried to maneuver things so he would end up with Zachary's property after his death even though Zachary had made it clear he had no intention of selling."

"And it looks as if the dirt on Kingston is not the only file Harriet had in the safe," Roy jumped in. "Here are the original documents relating to Kate's arrest and the subsequent scrubbing of her file."

"Where on earth did Harriet get all of this?" Jenna asked.

No one knew, but the documents in the safe were probably enough to give any number of people motive to blow up the town offices if they suspected Harriet had the documents hidden somewhere inside, but they didn't know where.

Kyle narrowed his gaze. "Harriet must have known she was playing with fire. I'm still not sure how she got ahold of these files, but given what we've found, I would say another conversation with Kingston is warranted."

"I agree. I'll track him down and see what he has to say for himself," Roy said.

# CHAPTER 28

Wednesday, November 22

As it turned out, Kingston had an answer for every question Roy threw at him. So, in the end, all Roy was able to deliver to the guy was a stern warning that he was onto him and was going to continue to dig. He also left him with the promise that he would be back and send him to prison if he was able to find the proof he needed to prove his theory. After Roy had talked to Kingston, and the two of us had discussed the situation in depth, we both agreed that, while James Kingston was bad news, he probably hadn't been the one to blow up the town hall and the town offices.

Which left us back to square one as far as I was concerned.

I decided to go back and look at everything we had uncovered to date. This included all the files Harriet had in the cloud, all the files we found in her home office, and all the files we'd found in the floor safe. After hours and hours of considering numerous suspects and numerous theories, I found that I'd settled on the simplest theory of all.

"Can I help you?" The tall, distinguished woman asked after I'd rung her bell.

"My name is Tj Jensen. I hoped I might speak to you about a story Harriet Kramer was working on before she died."

The woman pursed her lips but stepped aside. She led me down a long hallway to an elaborately decorated room. "I only have a few minutes. I have a book club meeting in just under an hour. We are having our monthly luncheon."

"I'll be brief," I promised.

The woman sat down across from me.

"I understand that before she died, Harriet found proof of what really happened to your husband."

Mrs. Edmonton nodded. "So she told me. I wasn't sure I believed her at the time, but in light of recent events, I can see that she knew what she was talking about."

"I understand that she informed you that your husband had not taken off as everyone seemed to think, but had, in fact, been murdered and buried in the foundation of the town hall."

"Yes, that is what she told me."

"When exactly did she tell you this?"

The woman glared at me. "I don't remember the exact date."

"Would you say it was a week or more prior to the explosion that eventually exposed your husband's remains?"

The woman leaned forward slightly. "What exactly is it that you are trying to ask me?"

"Did you blow up the town hall in order to prove that Harriet was right, and your husband was indeed buried there?"

The woman didn't answer, but I knew it was true.

"Innocent people died."

The woman's expression began to crumble. "I know. It wasn't supposed to happen that way. The man I hired to purchase and plant the bomb told me it would go off in the middle of the night. No one was supposed to get hurt." The woman looked me directly in the eye. "I swear to you. I didn't want to hurt anyone. I only wanted the money."

"Money?" I was expecting her to say she wanted justice or

closure or something, but money?

"The insurance money," The woman explained as she nervously pleated her skirt with her hands. "Before he died, my husband had been stealing from the bank in order to pay off a blackmailer who knew about the affair he'd been having. At the time, I didn't know this of course, but after he passed and I took over at the bank, I found the missing money and then was eventually able to track down the blackmailer, who'd fled the country by that point. While I was furious about what my husband had done, I was the most upset about the fact that the money was missing, and I had no way to replace it. I hoped that I would be able to use the twenty-million-dollar life insurance policy my husband had to make things right at the bank, but since there was no body or any proof at all that my husband was dead, the insurance company refused to pay. I can't tell you how hard it has been to keep the missing money a secret. I borrowed the money I needed to keep the bank running, and I've sold off most of our property other than this house, as well as most of my antiques and jewelry, just to make the payments. I am to the point where I have little else to sell and have been feeling desperate, and then Harriet came to me with the answers I needed. The insurance company told me in no uncertain terms that they needed a body in order for a payout to be possible, so I decided to provide them with a body." The woman swiped angrily at her tears. "I really didn't want anyone to die or to get hurt. I've done what I can to make it right, but I guess I can never make it right, can I?"

"No, I don't think you can. Are you the one who sent me the box of cash?"

The woman nodded. "I knew that the medical bills would provide a hardship for you and Mr. Warren. The others wouldn't be affected by the expense, but I wanted to do what I could for the two of you."

"I want to thank you for that, but I do need to call Deputy Fisher and tell him what I know."

The woman bowed her head. "I know. It's how it should be."

"Between you and me, I understand why you did what you did. I'm sorry about what happened to your husband. It should never have gone down that way, and hopefully, Deputy DuPont will spend a whole lot of years in prison for doing what he did."

The woman spoke in a tired voice. "I suppose bringing Robert's killer to justice is the silver lining in this whole mess."

# CHAPTER 29

Thursday, November 23

A house filled with people I loved made for just about a perfect day. The sun was high in the sky, the blue, blue lake shimmered outside the windows, the food was made to perfection, and everyone who showed up seemed to be relaxed and happy. As usual, Jenna was in the kitchen seeing to the last-minute details before the meal was served, and as usual, I could be found standing around watching her make the gravy.

"You always seem to be able to avoid lumps," I said, as I watched in amazement. "Every time I make gravy, there are lumps. A lot of them."

"That is because you just dump the flour in. You need to blend it slowly. Can you grab the pepper?"

"So did you talk to Dennis last night?" I asked after handing Jenna the pepper.

"I did."

"And?"

Jenna paused and looked at me. She hesitated, and then she turned back toward the gravy. "He was less than thrilled at first. I really wasn't surprised. He pointed out that we had new roads to travel and plans for the future that would be much harder with a child. I shared with him that I didn't disagree, but

I also shared that it really didn't matter. I reminded him that I was already pregnant. Debating whether or not it was a good idea to have another baby was moot at that point. We talked some more, and both agreed that what was done was done and we needed to find a way to deal with what existed rather than discussing the pros and cons of the situation. Dennis wanted me to take a second pregnancy test, just to be sure. I agreed that a second test might be a good idea. As we waited for the test to process, I found myself praying for another positive result. It was at that moment that I knew that in spite of my initial feeling of denial, I actually wanted this baby very much. When the test came out positive, I felt this intense joy, and I knew everything would be okay."

"And Dennis?"

"He is still working through things. I think he will be fine after he has a chance to get used to the idea. He loves the girls, and he loves being a father. He always wanted a son." Jenna put a hand on her stomach. "Maybe he'll finally get one."

"I hope so. I'm sure whether a boy or a girl, this baby is going to be awesome."

Jenna held her stirring spoon off to the side and hugged me with one arm. "I think so too."

Jenna returned to her gravy and Rosalie came in to check on the rolls. I had to admit she had done a fabulous job with them. They were light and airy and perfectly browned.

"The rolls turned out really good," I said, as I helped transfer them from cookie sheets to serving baskets. "And you made plenty for sandwiches."

"That was the plan. I'd love to have leftovers out at the resort tomorrow. Grandpa and I talked about inviting Doc and, of course, we would love it if you, Kyle, and the girls were there. Jenna and her family too if they want."

"I think that is a wonderful idea. I'll check with Kyle and

invite Jenna. As long as we are talking food, I thought we'd provide dinner for everyone who comes to the tree cutting on Saturday. Grandpa usually makes a huge pot of his famous spaghetti, but I realized that this year I should probably run our plans past you. You are, after all, the lady of the house now."

Rosalie smiled. "I appreciate that, but one of the reasons I love being part of your big wonderful family is because of all the traditions. I really wouldn't want to change a thing."

I reached out and hugged Rosalie. "And we are happy to have you as a part of the chaos."

Grandpa came up from behind and gave me a hug after Rosalie went in search of butter. "Great turn out," he said.

"It seems if as everyone made it just fine. I'm sorry about those who are not with us this year, but I'm glad to see that Bookman was feeling well enough to come." I glanced through the open space between the kitchen and dining room. "Helen seems to be doing better, as well."

"It feels odd to be having a big Thanksgiving dinner without Harriet. I just hope she is happy wherever she ended up and able to rest in peace. I felt like she never really did recover from Judge Harper's death."

"It hit all of us hard, but I have to agree that it seemed to hit her the hardest of all."

"The road back from what has happened is going to be a difficult one."

"It is. But Kyle and Jeff are working hard to get the town back in business, and Roy has assured me that he is doing everything he can to make sure that everyone involved in what happened will get exactly what they deserve."

"That's good, although I do feel bad about Mrs. Edmonton. I know what she did led to the death of two people, but I really don't think she meant to hurt anyone."

"I'm sure the court will take that into consideration.

Personally, I'm just happy that we were able to wrap things up before the holiday."

"Me too, pumpkin."

"So are you up to making your famous spaghetti this year for the tree cutting crowd?"

"I already bought the ingredients. I'll make the sauce tomorrow, so all we have to do on Saturday when we get back with the trees is make the noodles and the bread and salad."

"Just so you know, I'm going to invite Jenna and her family."

"I already spoke to Bookman, and he felt they would want to come to dinner, although he didn't feel up to the tree cutting part of the day. I figured we'd need some extra muscle this year, so I invited Jeff as well."

"That's a great idea. He has really stepped up to help Kyle since the explosion."

Kyle's mom called everyone into the dining room and instructed them to take their seats. Grandpa joined them, while Jenna poured the gravy into the gravy boats. Kyle came in to help with the last-minute chores, while the rest of the guests picked out seats and poured their beverage of choice.

"It looks like everything is ready," Jenna said, heading into the dining room with the gravy.

"So do we make our announcement or do we wait?" Kyle asked once we were alone.

I had to admit I was torn. "I don't know. Part of me wants to share our news with everyone, but I'm still not sure the girls are ready, and I did tell them I would wait until we had time to work out the details. What do you think?"

"Maybe we should wait. I want everyone to know how much I love you, but if there is a chance that the girls will be upset, I think we should wait. I really want them to be okay with this."

"I agree. We told our families and have plenty of time to tell everyone else."

Kyle took my hand in his. "Okay. Let's join our guests."

Kyle sat at the head of the table. I sat on one side, and Gracie sat on his other side. Ashley sat next to Kristi. Once everyone was seated, I thanked everyone for coming and suggested we go around the table and say what we were thankful for. I made a general statement about being thankful for friends and family. My dad said he was grateful for Rosalie, who had brought so much meaning into his life. Grandpa was grateful for Ashley and Gracie and the smile they brought him each morning. Ashley was grateful for Rosalie, who was teaching her to sew, and Frannie was grateful for friends that felt like family. Helen was grateful that Bookman was on the road to recovery, Doc was grateful for the same thing, Jenna was grateful for her family and the joy they brought to her life, and Dennis shared that he was grateful for wife and daughters, and the shared blessings he looked forward to in the following year. I glanced at Jenna, who seemed to only have eyes for the man sitting next to her and knew deep in my soul that they'd be okay. I smiled as each of our guests spoke until we finally made it around to Gracie, who was sitting next to Kyle. She didn't speak at first, which I had to admit had me worried, but eventually, she started in a soft voice.

"I'm grateful to Papa for giving me a home, and Rosalie for making Papa happy, and Grandpa for starting each day with a hot breakfast and warm hug, and I'm grateful for Ashley for being my sister, and Tj for being both my mom and my sister, and I'm especially grateful for Kyle who loves me and wants to marry Tj, so he can be my dad."

Everyone looked at Kyle and me. Kyle turned and hugged Gracie, who hugged him back.

"Marry Tj?" Helen asked. "Is there something the two of you want to share?"

Kyle glanced at me, and I nodded.

"Yes, Gracie is correct," I said. "Kyle and I are engaged."

Everyone who didn't already know about the engagement stopped to congratulate us.

"If you are engaged, where is your ring?" Kristi asked.

I was about to explain that we'd been waiting to make it official, when Kyle pushed back his chair, took a ring out of his pocket, and got down on one knee. "Tj Jensen, will you marry me?"

Before I could answer, Gracie spoke up with confusion evident in her voice. "I thought she was already going to marry you."

Kyle winked at her. "She was, but I think we should make it official."

"Say yes," Ashley whispered as she squirmed up and down in excitement.

"Yes," I said as Kyle slipped the ring on my finger, and everyone at the table broke into applause. "Yes, a million times, yes."

# KATHI DALEY

*USA Today* bestselling author Kathi Daley lives in beautiful Lake Tahoe with her husband, Ken. When she isn't writing, she likes spending time hiking the miles of desolate trails surrounding her home. She has authored more than seventy-five books in eight series including: Zoe Donovan Cozy Mysteries, Whales and Tails Island Mysteries, Sand and Sea Hawaiian Mysteries, Tj Jensen Paradise Lake Mysteries, Writer's Retreat Southern Seashore Mysteries, Rescue Alaska Paranormal Mysteries, and Seacliff High Teen Mysteries. Find out more about her books at www.kathidaley.com.

**The Tj Jensen Mystery Series
by Kathi Daley**

**Henery Press Mystery Books**

And finally, before you go...
Here are a few other mysteries
you might enjoy:

# NOT A CREATURE WAS STIRRING

Christina Freeburn

## A Merry & Bright Handcrafted Mystery (#1)

Empty nester Merry Winters loves three things: Christmas, crafting and her family. To regain purpose and joy, Merry hits the road to a Christmas vendor event with her furry sidekick Ebenezer in her new mobile crafting sleigh, aka an RV.

But it soon turns into the nightmare before Christmas when Merry unwraps her Scrooge of an ex-husband's body in one of the RV's compartments. Add to that his missing winning lottery ticket believed to be stashed somewhere in the RV, leading the homicide detective and Merry's stepdaughter to believe Merry is the one whodunit.

With visions of prison dancing in her head, will Merry be able to solve this Christmas calamity before she's locked away?

Available at booksellers nationwide and online

Visit www.henerypress.com for details

# THE HOUSE ON HALLOWED GROUND

Nancy Cole Silverman

## A Misty Dawn Mystery (#1)

When Misty Dawn, a former Hollywood Psychic to the Stars, moves into an old craftsman house, she encounters the former owner, the recently deceased Hollywood set designer, Wilson Thorne. Wilson is unaware of his circumstances, and when Misty explains the particulars of his limbo state, and how he might help himself if he helps her, he's not at all happy. That is until young actress Zoey Chamberlain comes to Misty's door for help.

Zoey has recently purchased The Pink Mansion and thinks it's haunted. But when Misty searches the house, it's not a ghost she finds, but a dead body. The police suspect Zoey, but Zoey fears the death may have been a result of the ghost...and a family curse. Together Misty and Wilson must untangle the secrets of The Pink Mansion or submit to the powers of the family curse.

Available at booksellers nationwide and online

Visit www.henerypress.com for details

# MURDER AT THE PALACE

Margaret Dumas

## A Movie Palace Mystery (#1)

Welcome to the Palace movie theater! Now Showing: Philandering husbands, ghostly sidekicks, and a murder or two.

When Nora Paige's movie-star husband leaves her for his latest co-star, she flees Hollywood to take refuge in San Francisco at the Palace, a historic movie theater that shows the classic films she loves. There she finds a band of misfit film buffs who care about movies (almost) as much as she does.

She also finds some shady financial dealings and the body of a murdered stranger. Oh, and then there's Trixie, the lively ghost of a 1930's usherette who appears only to Nora and has a lot to catch up on. With the help of her new ghostly friend, can Nora catch the killer before there's another murder at the Palace?

Available at booksellers nationwide and online

Visit www.henerypress.com for details

# BOARD STIFF

Kendel Lynn

## An Elliott Lisbon Mystery (#1)

As director of the Ballantyne Foundation on Sea Pine Island, SC, Elliott Lisbon scratches her detective itch by performing discreet inquiries for Foundation donors. Usually nothing more serious than retrieving a pilfered Pomeranian. Until Jane Hatting, Ballantyne board chair, is accused of murder. The Ballantyne's reputation tanks, Jane's headed to a jail cell, and Elliott's sexy ex is the new lieutenant in town.

Armed with moxie and her Mini Coop, Elliott uncovers a trail of blackmail schemes, gambling debts, illicit affairs, and investment scams. But the deeper she digs to clear Jane's name, the guiltier Jane looks. The closer she gets to the truth, the more treacherous her investigation becomes. With victims piling up faster than shells at a clambake, Elliott realizes she's next on the killer's list.

Available at booksellers nationwide and online

Visit www.henerypress.com for details